INSIGHT PUBLICA®

Nadakkave, Kozhikode, Kerala, India
+91 4954020666 | +91 9400737475
www.insightpublica.com | www.bookat.in
e-mail: insightpublica@gmail.com

Misalliance

Bernard Shaw

First Insight Edition: August 2019

ISBN 978-93-89155-55-6

Printed and Published by
InsightinPublica Printers & Publishers Pvt Ltd.

Misalliance
Bernard Shaw

Johnny Tarleton, an ordinary young business man of thirty or less, is taking his weekly Friday to Tuesday in the house of his father, John Tarleton, who has made a great deal of money out of Tarleton's Underwear. The house is in Surrey, on the slope of Hindhead; and Johnny, reclining, novel in hand, in a swinging chair with a little awning above it, is enshrined in a spacious half hemisphere of glass which forms a pavilion commanding the garden, and, beyond it, a barren but lovely landscape of hill profile with fir trees, commons of bracken and gorse, and wonderful cloud pictures. The glass pavilion springs from a bridgelike arch in the wall of the house, through which one comes into a big hall with tiled flooring, which suggests that the proprietor's notion of domestic luxury is founded on the lounges of weekend hotels. The arch is not quite in the centre of the wall. There is more wall to its right than to its left, and this space is occupied by a hat rack and umbrella stand in which tennis rackets, white parasols, caps, Panama hats, and other summery articles are bestowed. Just through the arch at this corner stands a new portable Turkish bath, recently unpacked, with its crate beside it, and on the crate the drawn nails and the hammer used in unpacking. Near the crate are open boxes of garden games: bowls and croquet. Nearly in the middle of the glass wall of the pavilion is a door giving on the garden, with a couple of steps to surmount the hot-water pipes which skirt the glass. At intervals round the pavilion are marble pillars with specimens of Viennese pottery on them, very flamboyant in colour and florid in design. Between them are folded garden chairs flung anyhow against the pipes. In the side walls are two doors: one near the hat stand, leading to the interior of the house, the other on the opposite side and at the other end, leading to the vestibule. There is no solid furniture except a sideboard which stands against the wall between the vestibule door and the pavilion, a small writing table with a blotter, a rack for telegram forms and stationery, and a wastepaper basket, standing out in the hall near the sideboard, and a lady's worktable, with two chairs at it, towards the other side of the lounge. The writing table has also two chairs at it. On the sideboard there is a tantalus, liqueur bottles, a syphon, a glass jug of lemonade, tumblers, and every convenience for casual drinking. Also a plate of sponge cakes, and a highly ornate punchbowl in the same style as the keramic display in the pavilion. Wicker chairs and little bamboo tables with ash trays and boxes of matches on them are scattered in all directions. In the pavilion, which is flooded with sunshine, is the elaborate patent swing seat and awning in which Johnny reclines with his novel. There are two wicker chairs right and left of him. Bentley Summerhays, one of those smallish, thinskinned youths, who from 17 to 70 retain unaltered the mental airs of the later and the physical appearance of the earlier age, appears in the garden and comes through the glass door into the pavilion. He is unmistakably a grade above Johnny socially; and though he looks sensitive enough, his assurance and his high voice are a little exasperating.

JOHNNY. Hallo! Wheres your luggage?

BENTLEY. I left it at the station. Ive walked up from Haslemere. [He goes to the hat stand and hangs up his hat].

JOHNNY [shortly] Oh! And who's to fetch it?

BENTLEY. Dont know. Dont care. Providence, probably. If not, your mother will have it fetched.

JOHNNY. Not her business, exactly, is it?

BENTLEY. [returning to the paviliohair on Johnny's right].

JOHNNY. [straightening up in the swing with a yell of protest] No. Now seriously, Bunny, Ive come down here to have a pleasant week-end; and I'm not going to stand your confounded arguments. If you want to argue, get out of this and go over to the Congregationalist minister's. He's a nailer at arguing. He likes it.

BENTLEY. You cant argue with a person when his livelihood depends on his not letting you convert him. And would you mind not calling me Bunny. My name is Bentley Summerhays, which you please.

JOHNNY. Whats the matter with Bunny?

BENTLEY. It puts me in a false position. Have you ever considered the fact that I was an afterthought?

JOHNNY. An afterthought? What do you mean by that?

BENTLEY. I—

JOHNNY. No, stop: I dont want to know. It's only a dodge to start an argument.

BENTLEY. Dont be afraid: it wont overtax your brain. My father was 44 when I was born. My mother was 41. There was twelve years between me and the next eldest. I was unexpected. I was probably unintentional. My brothers and sisters are not the least like me. Theyre the regular thing that you always get in the first batch from young parents: quite pleasant, ordinary, do-the-regular-thing sort: all body and no brains, like you.

JOHNNY. Thank you.

BENTLEY. Dont mention it, old chap. Now I'm different. By the time I was born, the old couple knew something. So I came out all brains and no more body than is absolutely necessary. I am really a good deal older than you, though you were born ten years sooner. Everybody feels that when they hear us talk; consequently, though it's quite natural to hear me calling you Johnny, it sounds ridiculous and unbecoming for you to call me Bunny. [He rises].

JOHNNY. Does it, by George? You stop me doing it if you can: thats all.

BENTLEY. If you go on doing it after Ive asked you not, youll feel an awful swine. [He strolls away carelessly to the sideboard with his eye on the sponge cakes]. At least I should; but I suppose youre not so particular.

JOHNNY [rising vengefully and following Bentley, who is forced to turn and listen] I'll tell you what it is, my boy: you want a good talking to; and I'm going to give it to you. If you think that because your father's a K.C.B., and you want to marry my sister, you can make yourself as nasty as you please and say what you like, youre mistaken. Let me tell you that except Hypatia, not one person in this house is in favor of her marrying you; and I dont believe shes happy about it herself. The match isnt settled yet: dont forget that. Youre on trial in the office because the Governor isnt giving his daughter money for an idle man to live on her. Youre on trial here because my mother thinks a girl should know what a man is like in the house before she marries him. Thats been going on for two months now; and whats the result? Youve got yourself thoroughly disliked in the office; and youre getting yourself thoroughly disliked here, all through your bad manners and your conceit, and the damned impudence you think clever.

BENTLEY. [deeply wounded and trying hard to control himself] Thats enough, thank you. You dont suppose, I hope, that I should have come down if I had known that that was how you felt about me. [He makes for the vestibule door].

JOHNNY. [collaring him]. No: you dont run away. I'm going to have this out with you. Sit down: d'y' hear? [Bentley attempts to go with dignity. Johnny slings him into a chair at the writing table, where he sits, bitterly humiliated, but afraid to speak lest he should burst into tears]. Thats the advantage of having more body than brains, you see: it enables me to teach you manners; and I'm going to do it too. Youre a spoilt young pup; and you need a jolly good licking. And if youre not careful youll get it: I'll see to that next time you call me a swine.

BENTLEY. I didnt call you a swine. But [bursting into a fury of tears] you are a swine: youre a beast: youre a brute: youre a cad: youre a liar: youre a bully: I should like to wring your damned neck for you.

JOHNNY. [with a derisive laugh] Try it, my son. [Bentley gives an inarticulate sob of rage]. Fighting isnt in your line. Youre too small and youre too childish. I always suspected that your cleverness wouldnt come to very much when it was brought up against something solid: some decent chap's fist, for instance.

BENTLEY. I hope your beastly fist may come up against a mad bull or a prizefighter's nose, or something solider than me. I dont care about your fist; but if everybody here dislikes me— [he is checked by a sob]. Well, I dont care. [Trying to recover himself] I'm sorry I intruded: I didnt know. [Breaking down again] Oh you beast! you pig! Swine, swine, swine, swine, swine! Now!

JOHNNY. All right, my lad, all right. Sling your mud as hard as you please: it wont stick to me. What I want to know is this. How is it that your father, who I suppose is the strongest man England has produced in our time—

BENTLEY. You got that out of your halfpenny paper. A lot you know about him!

JOHNNY. I dont set up to be able to do anything but admire him and appreciate him and be proud of him as an Englishman. If it wasnt for my respect for him, I wouldnt have stood your cheek for two days, let alone two months. But what I cant understand is why he didnt lick it out of you when you were a kid. For twenty-five years he kept a place twice as big as England in order: a place full of seditious coffee-colored heathens and pestilential white agitators in the middle of a lot of savage tribes. And yet he couldnt keep you in order. I dont set up to be half the man your father undoubtedly is; but, by George, it's lucky for you you were not my son. I dont hold with my own father's views about corporal punishment being wrong. It's necessary for some people; and I'd have tried it on you until you first learnt to howl and then to behave yourself.

BENTLEY. [contemptuously] Yes: behavior wouldnt come naturally to your son, would it?

JOHNNY. [stung into sudden violence] Now you keep a civil tongue in your head. I'll stand none of your snobbery. I'm just as proud of Tarleton's Underwear as you are of your father's title and his K.C.B., and all the rest of it. My father began in a little hole of a shop in Leeds no bigger than our pantry down the passage there. He—

BENTLEY. Oh yes: I know. Ive read it. "The Romance of Business, or The Story of Tarleton's Underwear. Please Take One!" I took one the day after I first met Hypatia. I went and bought half a dozen unshrinkable vests for her sake.

JOHNNY. Well: did they shrink?

BENTLEY. Oh, dont be a fool.

JOHNNY. Never mind whether I'm a fool or not. Did they shrink? Thats the point. Were they worth the money?

BENTLEY. I couldnt wear them: do you think my skin's as thick as your customers' hides? I'd as soon have dressed myself in a nutmeg grater.

JOHNNY. Pity your father didnt give your thin skin a jolly good lacing with a cane—!

BENTLEY. Pity you havnt got more than one idea! If you want to know, they did try that on me once, when I was a small kid. A silly governess did it. I yelled fit to bring down the house and went into convulsions and brain fever and that sort of thing for three weeks. So the old girl got the sack; and serve her right! After that, I was let do what I like. My father didnt want me to grow up a broken-spirited spaniel, which is your idea of a man, I suppose.

JOHNNY. Jolly good thing for you that my father made you come into the office and shew what you were made of. And it didnt come to much:

let me tell you that. When the Governor asked me where I thought we ought to put you, I said, "Make him the Office Boy." The Governor said you were too green. And so you were.

BENTLEY. I daresay. So would you be pretty green if you were shoved into my father's set. I picked up your silly business in a fortnight. Youve been at it ten years; and you havnt picked it up yet.

JOHNNY. Dont talk rot, child. You know you simply make me pity you.

BENTLEY. "Romance of Business" indeed! The real romance of Tarleton's business is the story that you understand anything about it. You never could explain any mortal thing about it to me when I asked you. "See what was done the last time": that was the beginning and the end of your wisdom. Youre nothing but a turnspit.

JOHNNY. A what!

BENTLEY. A turnspit. If your father hadnt made a roasting jack for you to turn, youd be earning twenty-four shillings a week behind a counter.

JOHNNY. If you dont take that back and apologize for your bad manners, I'll give you as good a hiding as ever—

BENTLEY. Help! Johnny's beating me! Oh! Murder! [He throws himself on the ground, uttering piercing yells].

JOHNNY. Dont be a fool. Stop that noise, will you. I'm not going to touch you. Sh—sh— Hypatia rushes in through the inner door, followed by Mrs Tarleton, and throws herself on her knees by Bentley. Mrs Tarleton, whose knees are stiffer, bends over him and tries to lift him. Mrs Tarleton is a shrewd and motherly old lady who has been pretty in her time, and is still very pleasant and likeable and unaffected. Hypatia is a typical English girl of a sort never called typical: that is, she has an opaque white skin, black hair, large dark eyes with black brows and lashes, curved lips, swift glances and movements that flash out of a waiting stillness, boundless energy and audacity held in leash.

HYPATIA. [pouncing on Bentley with no very gentle hand] Bentley: whats the matter? Dont cry like that: whats the use? Whats happened?

MRS TARLETON. Are you ill, child? [They get him up.] There, there, pet!

It's all right: dont cry [they put him into a chair]: there! there! there! Johnny will go for the doctor; and he'll give you something nice to make it well.

HYPATIA. What has happened, Johnny?

MRS TARLETON. Was it a wasp?

BENTLEY. [impatiently] Wasp be dashed!

MRS TARLETON. Oh Bunny! that was a naughty word.

BENTLEY. Yes, I know: I beg your pardon. [He rises, and extricates himself from them] Thats all right. Johnny frightened me. You know how easy it is to hurt me; and I'm too small to defend myself against Johnny.

MRS TARLETON. Johnny: how often have I told you that you must not bully the little ones. I thought youd outgrown all that.

HYPATIA. [angrily] I do declare, mamma, that Johnny's brutality makes it impossible to live in the house with him.

JOHNNY. [deeply hurt] It's twenty-seven years, mother, since you had that row with me for licking Robert and giving Hypatia a black eye because she bit me. I promised you then that I'd never raise my hand to one of them again; and Ive never broken my word. And now because this young whelp begins to cry out before he's hurt, you treat me as if I were a brute and a savage.

MRS TARLETON. No dear, not a savage; but you know you must not call our visitor naughty names.

BENTLEY. Oh, let him alone—

JOHNNY. [fiercely] Dont you interfere between my mother and me: d'y' hear?

HYPATIA. Johnny's lost his temper, mother. We'd better go. Come, Bentley.

MRS TARLETON. Yes: that will be best. [To Bentley] Johnny doesnt mean any harm, dear: he'll be himself presently. Come. The two ladies go out through the inner door with Bentley, who turns at the door to grin at Johnny as he goes out. Johnny, left alone, clenches his fists and grinds his teeth, but can find no relief in that way for his rage. After choking and stamping for a moment, he makes for the vestibule door. It opens before he reaches it; and Lord Summerhays comes in. Johnny glares at him, speechless. Lord Summerhays takes in the situation, and quickly takes the punchbowl from the sideboard and offers it to Johnny.

LORD SUMMERHAYS. Smash it. Dont hesitate: it's an ugly thing. Smash it: hard. [Johnny, with a stifled yell, dashes it in pieces, and then sits down and mops his brow]. Feel better now? [Johnny nods]. I know only one person alive who could drive me to the point of having either to break china or commit murder; and that person is my son Bentley. Was it he? [Johnny nods again, not yet able to speak]. As the car stopped I heard a yell which is only too familiar to me. It generally means that some infuriated person is trying to thrash Bentley. Nobody has ever succeeded, though almost everybody has tried. [He seats himself comfortably close to the writing table, and sets to work to collect the fragments of the punchbowl in the wastepaper basket whilst Johnny, with diminishing difficulty, collects himself]. Bentley is a problem which I confess I have never been able to solve. He was born to be a great success at the age of fifty. Most Englishmen of his class seem to be born to be great successes at the age of twenty-four at most. The domestic problem for me is how to endure Bentley until he is fifty. The problem for the nation is how to get itself governed by men whose growth is arrested when they are little more than college lads. Bentley doesnt really mean to be offensive. You can always make him cry by telling him you dont like him. Only, he cries so loud that the experiment should be made in the open air: in the middle of Salisbury Plain if possible. He has a hard and penetrating intellect and a remarkable power of looking facts in the face; but unfortunately, being very young, he has no idea of how very little of that sort of thing most of us can stand. On the other hand, he is frightfully sensitive and even affectionate; so that he probably gets as much as he gives in the way of hurt feelings. Youll excuse me rambling on like this about my son.

JOHNNY. [who has pulled himself together] You did it on purpose. I wasnt quite myself: I needed a moment to pull round: thank you.

LORD SUMMERHAYS. Not at all. Is your father at home?

JOHNNY. No: he's opening one of his free libraries. Thats another nice little penny gone. He's mad on reading. He promised another free library last week. It's ruinous. Itll hit you as well as me when Bunny marries Hypatia. When all Hypatia's money is thrown away on libraries, where will Bunny come in? Cant you stop him?

LORD SUMMERHAYS. I'm afraid not. Hes a perfect whirlwind. Indefatigable at public work. Wonderful man, I think.

JOHNNY. Oh, public work! He does too much of it. It's really a sort of laziness, getting away from your own serious business to amuse yourself with other people's. Mind: I dont say there isnt another side to it. It has its value as an advertisement. It makes useful acquaintances and leads to valuable business connections. But it takes his mind off the main chance; and he overdoes it.

LORD SUMMERHAYS. The danger of public business is that it never ends. A man may kill himself at it.

JOHNNY. Or he can spend more on it than it brings him in: thats how I look at it. What I say is that everybody's business is nobody's business. I hope I'm not a hard man, nor a narrow man, nor unwilling to pay reasonable taxes, and subscribe in reason to deserving charities, and even serve on a jury in my turn; and no man can say I ever refused to help a friend out of a difficulty when he was worth helping. But when you ask me to go beyond that, I tell you frankly I dont see it. I never did see it, even when I was only a boy, and had to pretend to take in all the ideas the Governor fed me up with. I didnt see it; and I dont see it.

LORD SUMMERHAYS. There is certainly no business reason why you should take more than your share of the world's work.

JOHNNY. So I say. It's really a great encouragement to me to find you agree with me. For of course if nobody agrees with you, how are you to know that youre not a fool?

LORD SUMMERHAYS. Quite so.

JOHNNY. I wish youd talk to him about it. It's no use my saying anything: I'm a child to him still: I have no influence. Besides, you know how to handle men. See how you handled me when I was making a fool of myself about Bunny!

LORD SUMMERHAYS. Not at all.

JOHNNY. Oh yes I was: I know I was. Well, if my blessed father had come in he'd have told me to control myself. As if I was losing my temper on purpose! Bentley returns, newly washed. He beams when he sees his father, and comes affectionately behind him and pats him on the shoulders.

BENTLEY. Hel-lo, commander! have you come? Ive been making a filthy silly ass of myself here. I'm awfully sorry, Johnny, old chap: I beg your pardon. Why dont you kick me when I go on like that?

LORD SUMMERHAYS. As we came through Godalming I thought I heard some yelling—

BENTLEY. I should think you did. Johnny was rather rough on me, though. He told me nobody here liked me; and I was silly enough to believe him.

LORD SUMMERHAYS. And all the women have been kissing you and pitying you ever since to stop your crying, I suppose. Baby!

BENTLEY. I did cry. But I always feel good after crying: it relieves my wretched nerves. I feel perfectly jolly now.

LORD SUMMERHAYS. Not at all ashamed of yourself, for instance?

BENTLEY. If I started being ashamed of myself I shouldnt have time for anything else all my life. I say: I feel very fit and spry. Lets all go down and meet the Grand Cham. [He goes to the hatstand and takes down his hat].

LORD SUMMERHAYS. Does Mr Tarleton like to be called the Grand Cham, do you think, Bentley?

BENTLEY. Well, he thinks hes too modest for it. He calls himself Plain John. But you cant call him that in his own office: besides, it doesnt suit him: it's not flamboyant enough.

JOHNNY. Flam what?

BENTLEY. Flamboyant. Lets go and meet him. Hes telephoned from Guildford to say hes on the road. The dear old son is always telephoning or telegraphing: he thinks hes hustling along like anything when hes only sending unnecessary messages.

LORD SUMMERHAYS. Thank you: I should prefer a quiet afternoon.

BENTLEY. Right O. I shant press Johnny: hes had enough of me for one week-end. [He goes out through the pavilion into the grounds].

JOHNNY. Not a bad idea, that.

LORD SUMMERHAYS. What?

JOHNNY. Going to meet the Governor. You know you wouldnt think it; but the Governor likes Bunny rather. And Bunny is cultivating it. I shouldnt be surprised if he thought he could squeeze me out one of these days.

LORD SUMMERHAYS. You dont say so! Young rascal! I want to consult you about him, if you dont mind. Shall we stroll over to the Gibbet? Bentley is too fast for me as a walking companion; but I should like a short turn.

JOHNNY. [rising eagerly, highly flattered] Right you are. Thatll suit me down to the ground. [He takes a Panama and stick from the hat stand]. Mrs Tarleton and Hypatia come back just as the two men are going out. Hypatia salutes Summerhays from a distance with an enigmatic lift of her eyelids in his direction and a demure nod before she sits down at the worktable and busies herself with her needle. Mrs Tarleton, hospitably fussy, goes over to him.

MRS TARLETON. Oh, Lord Summerhays, I didnt know you were here. Wont you have some tea?

LORD SUMMERHAYS. No, thank you: I'm not allowed tea. And I'm ashamed to say Ive knocked over your beautiful punch-bowl. You must let me replace it.

MRS TARLETON. Oh, it doesnt matter: I'm only too glad to be rid of it. The shopman told me it was in the best taste; but when my poor old nurse Martha got cataract, Bunny said it was a merciful provision of Nature to prevent her seeing our china.

LORD SUMMERHAYS. [gravely] That was exceedingly rude of Bentley, Mrs Tarleton. I hope you told him so.

MRS TARLETON. Oh, bless you! I dont care what he says; so long as he says it to me and not before visitors.

JOHNNY. We're going out for a stroll, mother.

MRS TARLETON. All right: dont let us keep you. Never mind about that crock: I'll get the girl to come and take the pieces away. [Recollecting herself] There! Ive done it again!

JOHNNY. Done what?

MRS TARLETON. Called her the girl. You know, Lord Summerhays, its a funny thing; but now I'm getting old, I'm dropping back into all the ways John and I had when we had barely a hundred a year. You should have known me when I was forty! I talked like a duchess; and if Johnny or Hypatia let slip a word that was like old times, I was down on them like anything. And now I'm beginning to do it myself at every turn.

LORD SUMMERHAYS. There comes a time when all that seems to matter so little. Even queens drop the mask when they reach our time of life.

MRS TARLETON. Let you alone for giving a thing a pretty turn! Youre a humbug, you know, Lord Summerhays. John doesnt know it; and Johnny doesnt know it; but you and I know it, dont we? Now thats something that even you cant answer; so be off with you for your walk without another word. Lord Summerhays smiles; bows; and goes out through the vestibule door, followed by Johnny. Mrs Tarleton sits down at the worktable and takes out her darning materials and one of her husband's socks. Hypatia is at the other side of the table, on her mother's right. They chat as they work.

HYPATIA. I wonder whether they laugh at us when they are by themselves!

MRS TARLETON. Who?

HYPATIA. Bentley and his father and all the toffs in their set.

MRS TARLETON. Oh, thats only their way. I used to think that the aristocracy were a nasty sneering lot, and that they were laughing at me and John. Theyre always giggling and pretending not to care much about anything. But you get used to it: theyre the same to one another and to everybody. Besides, what does it matter what they think? It's far worse when theyre civil, because that always means that they want you to lend them money; and you must never do that, Hypatia, because they never pay. How can they? They dont make anything, you see. Of course, if you can make up your mind to regard it as a gift, thats different; but then they generally ask you again; and you may as well say no first as last. You neednt be afraid of the aristocracy, dear: theyre only human creatures like ourselves after all; and youll hold your own with them easy enough.

HYPATIA. Oh, I'm not a bit afraid of them, I assure you.

MRS TARLETON. Well, no, not afraid of them, exactly; but youve got to pick up their ways. You know, dear, I never quite agreed with your father's notion of keeping clear of them, and sending you to a school that was so expensive that they couldnt afford to send their daughters there; so that all the girls belonged to big business families like ourselves. It takes all sorts to make a world; and I wanted you to see a little of all sorts. When you marry Bunny, and go among the women of his father's set, theyll shock you at first.

HYPATIA. [incredulously] How?

MRS TARLETON. Well, the things they talk about.

HYPATIA. Oh! scandalmongering?

MRS TARLETON. Oh no: we all do that: thats only human nature. But you know theyve no notion of decency. I shall never forget the first day I spent with a marchioness, two duchesses, and no end of Ladies This and That. Of course it was only a committee: theyd put me on to get a big subscription out of John. I'd never heard such talk in my life. The things they mentioned! And it was the marchioness that started it.

HYPATIA. What sort of things?

MRS TARLETON. Drainage!! She'd tried three systems in her castle; and she was going to do away with them all and try another. I didnt know which way to look when she began talking about it: I thought theyd all have got up and gone out of the room. But not a bit of it, if you please. They were all just as bad as she. They all had systems; and each of them swore by her own system. I sat there with my cheeks burning until one of the duchesses, thinking I looked out of it, I suppose, asked me what system I had. I said I was sure I knew nothing about such things, and hadnt we better change the subject. Then the fat was in the fire, I can tell you. There was a regular terror of a countess with an anaerobic system; and she told me, downright brutally, that I'd better learn something about them before my children died of diphtheria. That was just two months after I'd buried poor little Bobby; and that was the very thing he died of, poor little lamb! I burst out crying: I couldnt help it. It was as good as telling me I'd killed my own child. I had to go away; but before I was out of the door one of the duchesses—quite a young woman—began talking about what sour milk did in her inside and how she expected to live to be over a hundred if she took it regularly. And me listening to her, that had never dared to think that a duchess could have anything so common as an inside! I shouldnt have minded if it had been children's insides: we have to talk about them. But grown-up people! I was glad to get away that time.

HYPATIA. There was a physiology and hygiene class started at school; but of course none of our girls were let attend it.

MRS TARLETON. If it had been an aristocratic school plenty would have attended it. Thats what theyre like: theyve nasty minds. With really nice good women a thing is either decent or indecent; and if it's indecent, we just dont mention it or pretend to know about it; and theres an end of it. But all the aristocracy cares about is whether it can get any good out of the thing. Theyre what Johnny calls cynical-like. And of course nobody can say a word to them for it. Theyre so high up that they can do and say what they like.

HYPATIA. Well, I think they might leave the drains to their husbands. I shouldnt think much of a man that left such things to me.

MRS TARLETON. Oh, dont think that, dear, whatever you do. I never let on about it to you; but it's me that takes care of the drainage here. After what that countess said to me I wasnt going to lose another child or trust John. And I don't want my grandchildren to die any more than my children.

HYPATIA. Do you think Bentley will ever be as big a man as his father? I dont mean clever: I mean big and strong.

MRS TARLETON. Not he. Hes overbred, like one of those expensive little dogs. I like a bit of a mongrel myself, whether it's a man or a dog: theyre the best for everyday. But we all have our tastes: whats one woman's meat is another woman's poison. Bunny's a dear little fellow; but I never could have fancied him for a husband when I was your age.

HYPATIA. Yes; but he has some brains. Hes not like all the rest. One can't have everything.

MRS TARLETON. Oh, youre quite right, dear: quite right. It's a great thing to have brains: look what it's done for your father! Thats the reason I never said a word when you jilted poor Jerry Mackintosh.

HYPATIA. [excusing herself] I really couldnt stick it out with Jerry, mother. I know you liked him; and nobody can deny that hes a splendid animal—

MRS TARLETON. [shocked] Hypatia! How can you! The things that girls say nowadays!

HYPATIA. Well, what else can you call him? If I'd been deaf or he'd been dumb, I could have married him. But living with father, Ive got accustomed to cleverness. Jerry would drive me mad: you know very well hes a fool: even Johnny thinks him a fool.

MRS TARLETON. [up in arms at once in defence of her boy] Now dont begin about my Johnny. You know it annoys me. Johnny's as clever as anybody else in his own way. I dont say hes as clever as you in some ways; but hes a man, at all events, and not a little squit of a thing like your Bunny.

HYPATIA. Oh, I say nothing against your darling: we all know Johnny's perfection.

MRS TARLETON. Dont be cross, dearie. You let Johnny alone; and I'll let Bunny alone. I'm just as bad as you. There!

HYPATIA. Oh, I dont mind your saying that about Bentley. It's true. He is a little squit of a thing. I wish he wasnt. But who else is there? Think of all the other chances Ive had! Not one of them has as much brains in his whole body as Bentley has in his little finger. Besides, theyve no distinction. It's as much as I can do to tell one from the other. They wouldnt even have money if they werent the sons of their fathers, like Johnny. Whats a girl to do? I never met anybody like Bentley before. He may be small; but hes the best of the bunch: you cant deny that.

MRS TARLETON. [with a sigh] Well, my pet, if you fancy him, theres no more to be said. A pause follows this remark: the two women sewing silently.

HYPATIA. Mother: do you think marriage is as much a question of fancy as it used to be in your time and father's?

MRS TARLETON. Oh, it wasnt much fancy with me, dear: your father just wouldnt take no for an answer; and I was only too glad to be his wife instead of his shop-girl. Still, it's curious; but I had more choice than you in a way, because, you see, I was poor; and there are so many more poor men than rich ones that I might have had more of a pick, as you might say, if John hadnt suited me.

HYPATIA. I can imagine all sorts of men I could fall in love with; but I never seem to meet them. The real ones are too small, like Bunny, or too silly, like Jerry. Of course one can get into a state about any man: fall in love with him if you like to call it that. But who would risk marrying a man for love? I shouldnt. I remember three girls at school who agreed that the one man you should never marry was the man you were in love with, because it would make a perfect slave of you. Theres a sort of instinct against it, I think, thats just as strong as the other instinct. One of them, to my certain knowledge, refused a man she was in love with, and married another who was in love with her; and it turned out very well.

MRS TARLETON. Does all that mean that youre not in love with Bunny?

HYPATIA. Oh, how could anybody be in love with Bunny? I like him to kiss me just as I like a baby to kiss me. I'm fond of him; and he never bores me; and I see that hes very clever; but I'm not what you call gone about him, if thats what you mean.

MRS TARLETON. Then why need you marry him?

HYPATIA. What better can I do? I must marry somebody, I suppose. Ive realized that since I was twenty-three. I always used to take it as a matter of course that I should be married before I was twenty.

BENTLEY'S VOICE. [in the garden] Youve got to keep yourself fresh: to look at these things with an open mind.

JOHN TARLETON'S VOICE. Quite right, quite right: I always say so.

MRS TARLETON. Theres your father, and Bunny with him.

BENTLEY. Keep young. Keep your eye on me. Thats the tip for you. Bentley and Mr Tarleton (an immense and genial veteran of trade) come into view and enter the pavilion. JOHN

TARLETON. You think youre young, do you? You think I'm old? [energetically shaking off his motoring coat and hanging it up with his cap].

BENTLEY. [helping him with the coat] Of course youre old. Look at your face and look at mine. What you call your youth is nothing but your levity. Why do we get on so well together? Because I'm a young cub and youre an old josser. [He throws a cushion at Hypatia's feet and sits down on it with his back against her knees].

TARLETON. Old! Thats all you know about it, my lad. How do, Patsy! [Hypatia kisses him]. How is my Chickabiddy? [He kisses Mrs Tarleton's hand and poses expansively in the middle of the picture]. Look at me! Look at these wrinkles, these gray hairs, this repulsive mask that you call old age! What is it? [Vehemently] I ask you, what is it?

BENTLEY. Jolly nice and venerable, old man. Dont be discouraged.

TARLETON. Nice? Not a bit of it. Venerable? Venerable be blowed! Read your Darwin, my boy. Read your Weismann. [He goes to the sideboard for a drink of lemonade].

MRS TARLETON. For shame, John! Tell him to read his Bible.

TARLETON. [manipulating the syphon] Whats the use of telling children to read the Bible when you know they wont. I was kept away from the Bible for forty years by being told to read it when I was young. Then I picked it up one evening in a hotel in Sunderland when I had left all my papers in the train; and I found it wasnt half bad. [He drinks, and puts down the glass with a smack of enjoyment]. Better than most halfpenny papers, anyhow, if only you could make people believe it. [He sits down by the writing-table, near his wife]. But if you want to understand old age scientifically, read Darwin and Weismann. Of course if you want to understand it romantically, read about Solomon.

MRS TARLETON. Have you had tea, John?

TARLETON. Yes. Dont interrupt me when I'm improving the boy's mind. Where was I? This repulsive mask—Yes. [Explosively] What is death?

MRS TARLETON. John!

HYPATIA. Death is a rather unpleasant subject, papa.

TARLETON. Not a bit. Not scientifically. Scientifically it's a delightful subject. You think death's natural. Well, it isnt. You read Weismann. There wasnt any death to start with. You go look in any ditch outside and youll find swimming about there as fresh as paint some of the identical little live cells that Adam christened in the Garden of Eden. But if big things like us didnt die, we'd crowd one another off the face of the globe. Nothing survived, sir, except the sort of people that had the sense and good manners to die and make room for the fresh supplies. And so death was introduced by Natural Selection. You get it out of your head, my lad, that I'm going to die because I'm wearing out or decaying. Theres no such thing as decay to a vital man. I shall clear out; but I shant decay.

BENTLEY. And what about the wrinkles and the almond tree and the grasshopper that becomes a burden and the desire that fails?

TARLETON. Does it? by George! No, sir: it spiritualizes. As to your grasshopper, I can carry an elephant.

MRS TARLETON. You do say such things, Bunny! What does he mean by the almond tree?

TARLETON. He means my white hairs: the repulsive mask. That, my boy, is another invention of Natural Selection to disgust young women with me, and give the lads a turn.

MRS TARLETON. John: I wont have it. Thats a forbidden subject.

TARLETON. They talk of the wickedness and vanity of women painting their faces and wearing auburn wigs at fifty. But why shouldnt they? Why should a woman allow Nature to put a false mask of age on her when she knows that shes as young as ever? Why should she look in the glass and see a wrinkled lie when a touch of fine art will shew her a glorious truth? The wrinkles are a dodge to repel young men. Suppose she doesnt want to repel young men! Suppose she likes them!

MRS TARLETON. Bunny: take Hypatia out into the grounds for a walk: theres a good boy. John has got one of his naughty fits this evening.

HYPATIA. Oh, never mind me. I'm used to him.

BENTLEY. I'm not. I never heard such conversation: I cant believe my ears. And mind you, this is the man who objected to my marrying his daughter on the ground that a marriage between a member of the great and good middle class with one of the vicious and corrupt aristocracy would be a misalliance. A misalliance, if you please! This is the man Ive adopted as a father!

TARLETON. Eh! Whats that? Adopted me as a father, have you?

BENTLEY. Yes. Thats an idea of mine. I knew a chap named Joey Percival at Oxford (you know I was two months at Balliol before I was sent down for telling the old woman who was head of that silly college what I jolly well thought of him. He would have been glad to have me back, too, at the end of six months; but I wouldnt go: I just let him want; and serve him right!) Well, Joey was a most awfully clever fellow, and so nice! I asked him what made such a difference between him and all the other pups—they were pups, if you like. He told me it was very simple: they had only one father apiece; and he had three.

MRS TARLETON. Dont talk nonsense, child. How could that be?

BENTLEY. Oh, very simple. His father—

TARLETON. Which father?

BENTLEY. The first one: the regulation natural chap. He kept a tame philosopher in the house: a sort of Coleridge or Herbert Spencer kind of card, you know. That was the second father. Then his mother was an Italian princess; and she had an Italian priest always about. He was supposed to take charge of her conscience; but from what I could make out, she jolly well took charge of his. The whole three of them took charge of Joey's conscience. He used to hear them arguing like mad about everything. You see, the philosopher was a freethinker, and always believed the latest thing. The priest didnt believe anything, because it was sure to get him into trouble with someone or another. And the natural father kept an open mind and believed whatever paid him best. Between the lot of them Joey got cultivated no end. He said if he could only have had three mothers as well, he'd have backed himself against Napoleon.

TARLETON. [impressed] Thats an idea. Thats a most interesting idea: a most important idea.

MRS TARLETON. You always were one for ideas, John.

TARLETON. Youre right, Chickabiddy. What do I tell Johnny when he brags about Tarleton's Underwear? It's not the underwear. The underwear be hanged! Anybody can make underwear. Anybody can sell underwear. Tarleton's Ideas: thats whats done it. Ive often thought of putting that up over the shop.

BENTLEY. Take me into partnership when you do, old man. I'm wasted on the underwear; but I shall come in strong on the ideas.

TARLETON. You be a good boy; and perhaps I will.

MRS TARLETON. [scenting a plot against her beloved Johnny] Now, John: you promised—

TARLETON. Yes, yes. All right, Chickabiddy: dont fuss. Your precious Johnny shant be interfered with. [Bouncing up, too energetic to sit still] But I'm getting sick of that old shop. Thirty-five years Ive had of it: same blessed old stairs to go up and down every day: same old lot: same old game: sorry I ever started it now. I'll chuck it and try something else: something that will give a scope to all my faculties.

HYPATIA. Theres money in underwear: theres none in wild-cat ideas.

TARLETON. Theres money in me, madam, no matter what I go into.

MRS TARLETON. Dont boast, John. Dont tempt Providence.

TARLETON. Rats! You dont understand Providence. Providence likes to be tempted. Thats the secret of the successful man. Read Browning. Natural theology on an island, eh? Caliban was afraid to tempt Providence: that was why he was never able to get even with Prospero. What did Prospero do? Prospero didnt even tempt Providence: he was Providence. Thats one of Tarleton's ideas; and dont you forget it.

BENTLEY. You are full of beef today, old man.

TARLETON. Beef be blowed! Joy of life. Read Ibsen. [He goes into the pavilion to relieve his restlessness, and stares out with his hands thrust deep in his pockets].

HYPATIA. [thoughtful] Bentley: couldnt you invite your friend Mr Percival down here?

BENTLEY. Not if I know it. Youd throw me over the moment you set eyes on him.

MRS TARLETON. Oh, Bunny! For shame!

BENTLEY. Well, who'd marry me, dyou suppose, if they could get my brains with a full-sized body? No, thank you. I shall take jolly good care to keep Joey out of this until Hypatia is past praying for. Johnny and Lord Summerhays return through the pavilion from their stroll.

TARLETON. Welcome! welcome! Why have you stayed away so long?

LORD SUMMERHAYS. [shaking hands] Yes: I should have come sooner. But I'm still rather lost in England. [Johnny takes his hat and hangs it up beside his own]. Thank you. [Johnny returns to his swing and his novel. Lord Summerhays comes to the writing table]. The fact is that as Ive nothing to do, I never have time to go anywhere. [He sits down next Mrs Tarleton].

TARLETON. [following him and sitting down on his left] Paradox, paradox. Good. Paradoxes are the only truths. Read Chesterton. But theres lots for you to do here. You have a genius for government. You learnt your job out there in Jinghiskahn. Well, we want to be governed here in England. Govern us.

LORD SUMMERHAYS. Ah yes, my friend; but in Jinghiskahn you have to govern the right way. If you dont, you go under and come home. Here everything has to be done the wrong way, to suit governors who understand nothing but partridge shooting (our English native princes, in fact) and voters who dont know what theyre voting about. I dont understand these democratic games; and I'm afraid I'm too old to learn. What can I do but sit in the window of my club, which consists mostly of retired Indian Civil servants? We look on at the muddle and the folly and amateurishness; and we ask each other where a single fortnight of it would have landed us.

TARLETON. Very true. Still, Democracy's all right, you know. Read Mill. Read Jefferson.

LORD SUMMERHAYS. Yes. Democracy reads well; but it doesnt act well, like some people's plays. No, no, my friend Tarleton: to make Democracy work, you need an aristocratic democracy. To make Aristocracy work, you need a democratic aristocracy. Youve got neither; and theres an end of it.

TARLETON. Still, you know, the superman may come. The superman's an idea. I believe in ideas. Read Whatshisname.

LORD SUMMERHAYS. Reading is a dangerous amusement, Tarleton. I wish I could persuade your free library people of that.

TARLETON. Why, man, it's the beginning of education.

LORD SUMMERHAYS. On the contrary, it's the end of it. How can you dare teach a man to read until youve taught him everything else first?

JOHNNY. [intercepting his father's reply by coming out of the swing and taking the floor] Leave it at that. Thats good sense. Anybody on for a game of tennis?

BENTLEY. Oh, lets have some more improving conversation. Wouldnt you rather, Johnny?

JOHNNY. If you ask me, no.

TARLETON. Johnny: you dont cultivate your mind. You dont read.

JOHNNY. [coming between his mother and Lord Summerhays, book in hand] Yes I do. I bet you what you like that, page for page, I read more than you, though I dont talk about it so much. Only, I dont read the same books. I like a book with a plot in it. You like a book with nothing in it but some idea that the chap that writes it keeps worrying, like a cat chasing its own tail. I can stand a little of it, just as I can stand watching the cat for two minutes, say, when Ive nothing better to do. But a man soon gets fed up with that sort of thing. The fact is, you look on an author as a sort of god. I look on him as a man that I pay to do a certain thing for me. I pay him to amuse me and to take me out of myself and make me forget.

TARLETON. No. Wrong principle. You want to remember. Read Kipling. "Lest we forget."

JOHNNY. If Kipling wants to remember, let him remember. If he had to run Tarleton's Underwear, he'd be jolly glad to forget. As he has a much softer job, and wants to keep himself before the public, his cry is, "Dont you forget the sort of things I'm rather clever at writing about." Well, I dont blame him: it's his business: I should do the same in his place. But what he wants and what I want are two different things. I want to forget; and I pay another man to make me forget. If I buy a book or go to the theatre, I want to forget the shop and forget myself from the moment I go in to the moment I come out. Thats what I pay my money for. And if I find that the author's simply getting at me the whole time, I consider that hes obtained my money under false pretences. I'm not a morbid crank: I'm a natural man; and, as such, I dont like being got at. If a man in my employment did it, I should sack him. If a member of my club did it, I should cut him. If he went too far with it, I should bring his conduct before the committee. I might even punch his head, if it came to that. Well, who and what is an author that he should be privileged to take liberties that are not allowed to other men?

MRS TARLETON. You see, John! What have I always told you? Johnny has as much to say for himself as anybody when he likes.

JOHNNY. I'm no fool, mother, whatever some people may fancy. I dont set up to have as many ideas as the Governor; but what ideas I have are consecutive, at all events. I can think as well as talk.

BENTLEY. [to Tarleton, chuckling] Had you there, old man, hadnt he? You are rather all over the shop with your ideas, aint you?

JOHNNY. [handsomely] I'm not saying anything against you, Governor. But I do say that the time has come for sane, healthy, unpretending men like me to make a stand against this conspiracy of the writing and talking and artistic lot to put us in the back row. It isnt a fact that we're inferior to them: it's a put-up job; and it's they that have put the job up. It's we that run the country for them; and all the thanks we get is to be told we're Philistines and vulgar tradesmen and sordid city men and so forth, and that theyre all angels of light and leading. The time has come to assert ourselves and put a stop to their stuck-up nonsense. Perhaps if we had nothing better to do than talking or writing, we could do it better than they. Anyhow, theyre the failures and refuse of business (hardly a man of them that didnt begin in an office) and we're the successes of it. Thank God I havnt failed yet at anything; and I dont believe I should fail at literature if it would pay me to turn my hand to it.

BENTLEY. Hear, hear!

MRS TARLETON. Fancy you writing a book, Johnny! Do you think he could, Lord Summerhays?

LORD SUMMERHAYS. Why not? As a matter of fact all the really prosperous authors I have met since my return to England have been very like him.

TARLETON. [again impressed] Thats an idea. Thats a new idea. I believe I ought to have made Johnny an author. Ive never said so before for fear of hurting his feelings, because, after all, the lad cant help it; but Ive never thought Johnny worth tuppence as a man of business.

JOHNNY. [sarcastic] Oh! You think youve always kept that to yourself, do you, Governor? I know your opinion of me as well as you know it yourself. It takes one man of business to appreciate another; and you arnt, and you never have been, a real man of business. I know where Tarleton's would have been three of four times if it hadnt been for me. [With a snort and a nod to emphasize the implied warning, he retreats to the Turkish bath, and lolls against it with an air of good-humoured indifference].

TARLETON. Well, who denies it? Youre quite right, my boy. I don't mind confessing to you all that the circumstances that condemned me to keep a shop are the biggest tragedy in modern life. I ought to have been a writer. I'm essentially a man of ideas. When I was a young man I sometimes used to pray that I might fail, so that I should be justified in giving up business and doing something: something first-class. But it was no good: I couldnt fail. I said to myself that if I could only once go to my Chickabiddy here and shew her a chartered accountant's statement proving that I'd made 20 pounds less than last year, I could ask her to let me chance Johnny's and Hypatia's future by going into literature. But it was no good. First it was 250 pounds more than last year. Then it was 700 pounds. Then it was 2000 pounds. Then I saw it was no use: Prometheus was chained to his rock: read Shelley: read Mrs Browning. Well, well, it was not to be. [He rises solemnly]. Lord Summerhays: I ask you to excuse me for a few moments. There are times when a man needs to meditate in solitude on his destiny. A chord is touched; and he sees the drama of his life as a spectator sees a play. Laugh if you feel inclined: no man sees the comic side of it more than I. In the theatre of life everyone may be amused except the actor. [Brightening] Theres an idea in this: an idea for a picture. What a pity young Bentley is not a painter! Tarleton meditating on his destiny. Not in a toga. Not in the trappings of the tragedian or the philosopher. In plain coat and trousers: a man like any other man. And beneath that coat and trousers a human soul. Tarleton's Underwear! [He goes out gravely into the vestibule].

MRS TARLETON. [fondly] I suppose it's a wife's partiality, Lord Summerhays; but I do think John is really great. I'm sure he was meant to be a king. My father looked down on John, because he was a rate collector, and John kept a shop. It hurt his pride to have to borrow money so often from John; and he used to console himself by saying, "After all, he's only a linendraper." But at last one day he said to me, "John is a king."

BENTLEY. How much did he borrow on that occasion?

LORD SUMMERHAYS. [sharply] Bentley!

MRS TARLETON. Oh, dont scold the child: he'd have to say something like that if it was to be his last word on earth. Besides, hes quite right: my poor father had asked for his usual five pounds; and John gave him a hundred in his big way. Just like a king.

LORD SUMMERHAYS. Not at all. I had five kings to manage in Jinghiskahn; and I think you do your husband some injustice, Mrs Tarleton. They pretended to like me because I kept their brothers from murdering them; but I didnt like them. And I like Tarleton.

MRS TARLETON. Everybody does. I really must go and make the cook do him a Welsh rabbit. He expects one on special occasions. [She goes to the inner door]. Johnny: when he comes back ask him where we're to put that new Turkish bath. Turkish baths are his latest. [She goes out].

JOHNNY. [coming forward again] Now that the Governor has given himself away, and the old lady's gone, I'll tell you something, Lord Summerhays. If you study men whove made an enormous pile in business without being keen on money, youll find that they all have a slate off. The Governor's a wonderful man; but hes not quite all there, you know. If you notice, hes different from me; and whatever my failings may be, I'm a sane man. Erratic: thats what he is. And the danger is that some day he'll give the whole show away.

LORD SUMMERHAYS. Giving the show away is a method like any other method. Keeping it to yourself is only another method. I should keep an open mind about it.

JOHNNY. Has it ever occurred to you that a man with an open mind must be a bit of a scoundrel? If you ask me, I like a man who makes up his mind once for all as to whats right and whats wrong and then sticks to it. At all events you know where to have him.

LORD SUMMERHAYS. That may not be his object.

BENTLEY. He may want to have you, old chap.

JOHNNY. Well, let him. If a member of my club wants to steal my umbrella, he knows where to find it. If a man put up for the club who had an open mind on the subject of property in umbrellas, I should blackball him. An open mind is all very well in clever talky-talky; but in conduct and in business give me solid ground.

LORD SUMMERHAYS. Yes: the quicksands make life difficult. Still, there they are. It's no use pretending theyre rocks.

JOHNNY. I dont know. You can draw a line and make other chaps toe it. Thats what I call morality.

LORD SUMMERHAYS. Very true. But you dont make any progress when youre toeing a line.

HYPATIA. [suddenly, as if she could bear no more of it] Bentley: do go and play tennis with Johnny. You must take exercise.

LORD SUMMERHAYS. Do, my boy, do. [To Johnny] Take him out and make him skip about.

BENTLEY. [rising reluctantly] I promised you two inches more round my chest this summer. I tried exercises with an indiarubber expander; but I wasnt strong enough: instead of my expanding it, it crumpled me up. Come along, Johnny.

JOHNNY. Do you no end of good, young chap. [He goes out with Bentley through the pavilion]. Hypatia throws aside her work with an enormous sigh of relief.

LORD SUMMERHAYS. At last!

HYPATIA. At last. Oh, if I might only have a holiday in an asylum for the dumb. How I envy the animals! They cant talk. If Johnny could only put back his ears or wag his tail instead of laying down the law, how much better it would be! We should know when he was cross and when he was pleased; and thats all we know now, with all his talk. It never stops: talk, talk, talk, talk. Thats my life. All the day I listen to mamma talking; at dinner I listen to papa talking; and when papa stops for breath I listen to Johnny talking.

LORD SUMMERHAYS. You make me feel very guilty. I talk too, I'm afraid.

HYPATIA. Oh, I dont mind that, because your talk is a novelty. But it must have been dreadful for your daughters.

LORD SUMMERHAYS. I suppose so.

HYPATIA. If parents would only realize how they bore their children! Three or four times in the last half hour Ive been on the point of screaming.

LORD SUMMERHAYS. Were we very dull?

HYPATIA. Not at all: you were very clever. Thats whats so hard to bear, because it makes it so difficult to avoid listening. You see, I'm young; and I do so want something to happen. My mother tells me that when I'm her age, I shall be only too glad that nothing's happened; but I'm not her age; so what good is that to me? Theres my father in the garden, meditating on his destiny. All very well for him: hes had a destiny to meditate on; but I havnt had any destiny yet. Everything's happened to him: nothing's happened to me. Thats why this unending talk is so maddeningly uninteresting to me.

LORD SUMMERHAYS. It would be worse if we sat in silence.

HYPATIA. No it wouldnt. If you all sat in silence, as if you were waiting for something to happen, then there would be hope even if nothing did happen. But this eternal cackle, cackle, cackle about things in general is only fit for old, old, OLD people. I suppose it means something to them: theyve had their fling. All I listen for is some sign of it ending in something; but just when it seems to be coming to a point, Johnny or papa just starts another hare; and it all begins over again; and I realize that it's never going to lead anywhere and never going to stop. Thats when I want to scream. I wonder how you can stand it.

LORD SUMMERHAYS. Well, I'm old and garrulous myself, you see. Besides, I'm not here of my own free will, exactly. I came because you ordered me to come.

HYPATIA. Didnt you want to come?

LORD SUMMERHAYS. My dear: after thirty years of managing other people's business, men lose the habit of considering what they want or dont want.

HYPATIA. Oh, dont begin to talk about what men do, and about thirty years experience. If you cant get off that subject, youd better send for Johnny and papa and begin it all over again.

LORD SUMMERHAYS. I'm sorry. I beg your pardon.

HYPATIA. I asked you, didnt you want to come?

LORD SUMMERHAYS. I did not stop to consider whether I wanted or not, because when I read your letter I knew I had to come.

HYPATIA. Why?

LORD SUMMERHAYS. Oh come, Miss Tarleton! Really, really! Dont force me to call you a blackmailer to your face. You have me in your power; and I do what you tell me very obediently. Dont ask me to pretend I do it of my own free will.

HYPATIA. I dont know what a blackmailer is. I havnt even that much experience.

LORD SUMMERHAYS. A blackmailer, my dear young lady, is a person who knows a disgraceful secret in the life of another person, and extorts money from that other person by threatening to make his secret public unless the money is paid.

HYPATIA. I havnt asked you for money.

LORD SUMMERHAYS. No; but you asked me to come down here and talk to you; and you mentioned casually that if I didnt youd have nobody to talk about me to but Bentley. That was a threat, was it not?

HYPATIA. Well, I wanted you to come.

LORD SUMMERHAYS. In spite of my age and my unfortunate talkativeness?

HYPATIA. I like talking to you. I can let myself go with you. I can say things to you I cant say to other people.

LORD SUMMERHAYS. I wonder why?

HYPATIA. Well, you are the only really clever, grown-up, high-class, experienced man I know who has given himself away to me by making an utter fool of himself with me. You cant wrap yourself up in your toga after that. You cant give yourself airs with me.

LORD SUMMERHAYS. You mean you can tell Bentley about me if I do.

HYPATIA. Even if there wasnt any Bentley: even if you didnt care (and I really dont see why you should care so much) still, we never could be on conventional terms with one another again. Besides, Ive got a feeling for you: almost a ghastly sort of love for you.

LORD SUMMERHAYS. [shrinking] I beg you—no, please.

HYPATIA. Oh, it's nothing at all flattering: and, of course, nothing wrong, as I suppose youd call it.

LORD SUMMERHAYS. Please believe that I know that. When men of my age—

HYPATIA. [impatiently] Oh, do talk about yourself when you mean yourself, and not about men of your age.

LORD SUMMERHAYS. I'll put it as bluntly as I can. When, as you say, I made an utter fool of myself, believe me, I made a poetic fool of myself. I was seduced, not by appetites which, thank Heaven, Ive long outlived: not even by the desire of second childhood for a child companion, but by the innocent impulse to place the delicacy and wisdom and spirituality of my age at the affectionate service of your youth for a few years, at the end of which you would be a grown, strong, formed—widow. Alas, my dear, the delicacy of age reckoned, as usual, without the derision and cruelty of youth. You told me that you didnt want to be an old man's nurse, and that you didnt want to have undersized children like Bentley. It served me right: I dont reproach you: I was an old fool. But how you can imagine, after that, that I can suspect you of the smallest feeling for me except the inevitable feeling of early youth for late age, or imagine that I have any feeling for you except one of shrinking humiliation, I cant understand.

HYPATIA. I dont blame you for falling in love with me. I shall be grateful to you all my life for it, because that was the first time that anything really interesting happened to me.

LORD SUMMERHAYS. Do you mean to tell me that nothing of that kind had ever happened before? that no man had ever—

HYPATIA. Oh, lots. Thats part of the routine of life here: the very dullest part of it. The young man who comes a-courting is as familiar an incident in my life as coffee for breakfast. Of course, hes too much of a gentleman to misbehave himself; and I'm too much of a lady to let him; and hes shy and sheepish; and I'm correct and self-possessed; and at last, when I can bear it no longer, I either frighten him off, or give him a chance of proposing, just to see how he'll do it, and refuse him because he does it in the same silly way as all the rest. You dont call that an event in one's life, do you? With you it was different. I should as soon have expected the North Pole to fall in love with me as you. You know I'm only a linen-draper's daughter when all's said. I was afraid of you: you, a great man! a lord! and older than my father. And then what a situation it was! Just think of it! I was engaged to your son; and you knew nothing about it. He was afraid to tell you: he brought you down here because he thought if he could throw us together I could get round you because I was such a ripping girl. We arranged it all: he and I. We got Papa and Mamma and Johnny out of the way splendidly; and then Bentley took himself off, and left us—you and me!—to take a walk through the heather and admire the scenery of Hindhead. You never dreamt that it was all a plan: that what made me so nice was the way I was playing up to my destiny as the sweet girl that was to make your boy happy. And then! and then! [She rises to dance and clap her hands in her glee].

LORD SUMMERHAYS. [shuddering] Stop, stop. Can no woman understand a man's delicacy?

HYPATIA. [revelling in the recollection] And then—ha, ha!—you proposed. You! A father! For your son's girl!

LORD SUMMERHAYS. Stop, I tell you. Dont profane what you dont understand.

HYPATIA. That was something happening at last with a vengeance. It was splendid. It was my first peep behind the scenes. If I'd been seventeen I should have fallen in love with you. Even as it is, I feel quite differently towards you from what I do towards other old men. So [offering her hand] you may kiss my hand if that will be any fun for you.

LORD SUMMERHAYS. [rising and recoiling to the table, deeply revolted] No, no, no. How dare you? [She laughs mischievously]. How callous youth is! How coarse! How cynical! How ruthlessly cruel!

HYPATIA. Stuff! It's only that youre tired of a great many things Ive never tried.

LORD SUMMERHAYS. It's not alone that. Ive not forgotten the brutality of my own boyhood. But do try to learn, glorious young beast that you are, that age is squeamish, sentimental, fastidious. If you cant understand my holier feelings, at least you know the bodily infirmities of the old. You know that I darent eat all the rich things you gobble up at every meal; that I cant bear the noise and racket and clatter that affect you no more than they affect a stone. Well, my soul is like that too. Spare it: be gentle with it [he involuntarily puts out his hands to plead: she takes them with a laugh]. If you could possibly think of me as half an angel and half an invalid, we should get on much better together.

HYPATIA. We get on very well, I think. Nobody else ever called me a glorious young beast. I like that. Glorious young beast expresses exactly what I like to be.

LORD SUMMERHAYS. [extricating his hands and sitting down] Where on earth did you get these morbid tastes? You seem to have been well brought up in a normal, healthy, respectable, middle-class family. Yet you go on like the most unwholesome product of the rankest Bohemianism.

HYPATIA. Thats just it. I'm fed up with—

LORD SUMMERHAYS. Horrible expression. Dont.

HYPATIA. Oh, I daresay it's vulgar; but theres no other word for it. I'm fed up with nice things: with respectability, with propriety! When a woman has nothing to do, money and respectability mean that nothing is ever allowed to happen to her. I dont want to be good; and I dont want to be bad: I just dont want to be bothered about either good or bad: I want to be an active verb.

LORD SUMMERHAYS. An active verb? Oh, I see. An active verb signifies to be, to do, or to suffer.

HYPATIA. Just so: how clever of you! I want to be; I want to do; and I'm game to suffer if it costs that. But stick here doing nothing but being good and nice and ladylike I simply wont. Stay down here with us for a week; and I'll shew you what it means: shew it to you going on day after day, year after year, lifetime after lifetime.

LORD SUMMERHAYS. Shew me what?

HYPATIA. Girls withering into ladies. Ladies withering into old maids. Nursing old women. Running errands for old men. Good for nothing else at last. Oh, you cant imagine the fiendish selfishness of the old people and the maudlin sacrifice of the young. It's more unbearable than any poverty: more horrible than any regular-right-down wickedness. Oh, home! home! parents! family! duty! how I loathe them! How I'd like to see them all blown to bits! The poor escape. The wicked escape. Well, I cant be poor: we're rolling in money: it's no use pretending we're not. But I can be wicked; and I'm quite prepared to be.

LORD SUMMERHAYS. You think that easy?

HYPATIA. Well, isnt it? Being a man, you ought to know.

LORD SUMMERHAYS. It requires some natural talent, which can no doubt be cultivated. It's not really easy to be anything out of the common.

HYPATIA. Anyhow, I mean to make a fight for living.

LORD SUMMERHAYS. Living your own life, I believe the Suffragist phrase is.

HYPATIA. Living any life. Living, instead of withering without even a gardener to snip you off when youre rotten.

LORD SUMMERHAYS. Ive lived an active life; but Ive withered all the same.

HYPATIA. No: youve worn out: thats quite different. And youve some life in you yet or you wouldnt have fallen in love with me. You can never imagine how delighted I was to find that instead of being the correct sort of big panjandrum you were supposed to be, you were really an old rip like papa.

LORD SUMMERHAYS. No, no: not about your father: I really cant bear it. And if you must say these terrible things: these heart-wounding shameful things, at least find something prettier to call me than an old rip.

HYPATIA. Well, what would you call a man proposing to a girl who might be—

LORD SUMMERHAYS. His daughter: yes, I know.

HYPATIA. I was going to say his granddaughter.

LORD SUMMERHAYS. You always have one more blow to get in.

HYPATIA. Youre too sensitive. Did you ever make mud pies when you were a kid—beg pardon: a child.

LORD SUMMERHAYS. I hope not.

HYPATIA. It's a dirty job; but Johnny and I were vulgar enough to like it. I like young people because theyre not too afraid of dirt to live. Ive grown out of the mud pies; but I like slang; and I like bustling you up by saying things that shock you; and I'd rather put up with swearing and smoking than with dull respectability; and there are lots of things that would just shrivel you up that I think rather jolly. Now!

LORD SUMMERHAYS. Ive not the slightest doubt of it. Dont insist.

HYPATIA. It's not your ideal, is it?

LORD SUMMERHAYS. No.

HYPATIA. Shall I tell you why? Your ideal is an old woman. I daresay shes got a young face; but shes an old woman. Old, old, old. Squeamish. Cant stand up to things. Cant enjoy things: not real things. Always on the shrink.

LORD SUMMERHAYS. On the shrink! Detestable expression.

HYPATIA. Bah! you cant stand even a little thing like that. What good are you? Oh, what good are you?

LORD SUMMERHAYS. Dont ask me. I dont know. I dont know. Tarleton returns from the vestibule. Hypatia sits down demurely.

HYPATIA. Well, papa: have you meditated on your destiny?

TARLETON. [puzzled] What? Oh! my destiny. Gad, I forgot all about it: Jock started a rabbit and put it clean out of my head. Besides, why should I give way to morbid introspection? It's a sign of madness. Read Lombroso. [To Lord Summerhays] Well, Summerhays, has my little girl been entertaining you?

LORD SUMMERHAYS. Yes. She is a wonderful entertainer.

TARLETON. I think my idea of bringing up a young girl has been rather a success. Dont you listen to this, Patsy: it might make you conceited. Shes never been treated like a child. I always said the same thing to her mother. Let her read what she likes. Let her do what she likes. Let her go where she likes. Eh, Patsy?

HYPATIA. Oh yes, if there had only been anything for me to do, any place for me to go, anything I wanted to read.

TARLETON. There, you see! Shes not satisfied. Restless. Wants things to happen. Wants adventures to drop out of the sky.

HYPATIA. [gathering up her work] If youre going to talk about me and my education, I'm off.

TARLETON. Well, well, off with you. [To Lord Summerhays] Shes active, like me. She actually wanted me to put her into the shop.

HYPATIA. Well, they tell me that the girls there have adventures sometimes. [She goes out through the inner door]

TARLETON. She had me there, though she doesnt know it, poor innocent lamb! Public scandal exaggerates enormously, of course; but moralize as you will, superabundant vitality is a physical fact that cant be talked away. [He sits down between the writing table and the sideboard]. Difficult question this, of bringing up children. Between ourselves, it has beaten me. I never was so surprised in my life as when I came to know Johnny as a man of business and found out what he was really like. How did you manage with your sons?

LORD SUMMERHAYS. Well, I really hadnt time to be a father: thats the plain truth of the matter. Their poor dear mother did the usual thing while they were with us. Then of course, Harrow, Cambridge, the usual routine of their class. I saw very little of them, and thought very little about them: how could I? with a whole province on my hands. They and I are—acquaintances. Not perhaps, quite ordinary acquaintances: theres a sort of—er—I should almost call it a sort of remorse about the way we shake hands (when we do shake hands) which means, I suppose, that we're sorry we dont care more for one another; and I'm afraid we dont meet oftener than we can help. We put each other too much out of countenance. It's really a very difficult relation. To my mind not altogether a natural one.

TARLETON. [impressed, as usual] Thats an idea, certainly. I dont think anybody has ever written about that.

LORD SUMMERHAYS. Bentley is the only one who was really my son in any serious sense. He was completely spoilt. When he was sent to a preparatory school he simply yelled until he was sent home. Harrow was out of the question; but we managed to tutor him into Cambridge. No use: he was sent down. By that time my work was over; and I saw a good deal of him. But I could do nothing with him—except look on. I should have thought your case was quite different. You keep up the middle-class tradition: the day school and the business training instead of the university. I believe in the day school part of it. At all events, you know your own children.

TARLETON. Do you? I'm not so sure of it. Fact is, my dear Summerhays, once childhood is over, once the little animal has got past the stage at which it acquires what you might call a sense of decency, it's all up with the relation between parent and child. You cant get over the fearful shyness of it.

LORD SUMMERHAYS. Shyness?

TARLETON. Yes, shyness. Read Dickens.

LORD SUMMERHAYS [surprised] Dickens!! Of all authors, Charles Dickens! Are you serious?

TARLETON. I dont mean his books. Read his letters to his family. Read any man's letters to his children. Theyre not human. Theyre not about himself or themselves. Theyre about hotels, scenery, about the weather, about getting wet and losing the train and what he saw on the road and all that. Not a word about himself. Forced. Shy. Duty letters. All fit to be published: that says everything. I tell you theres a wall ten feet thick and ten miles high between parent and child. I know what I'm talking about. Ive girls in my employment: girls and young men. I had ideas on the subject. I used to go to the parents and tell them not to let their children go out into the world without instruction in the dangers and temptations they were going to be thrown into. What did every one of the mothers say to me? "Oh, sir, how could I speak of such things to my own daughter?" The men said I was quite right; but they didnt do it, any more than I'd been able to do it myself to Johnny. I had to leave books in his way; and I felt just awful when I did it. Believe me, Summerhays, the relation between the young and the old should be an innocent relation. It should be something they could talk about. Well, the relation between parent and child may be an affectionate relation. It may be a useful relation. It may be a necessary relation. But it can never be an innocent relation. Youd die rather than allude to it. Depend on it, in a thousand years itll be considered bad form to know who your father and mother are. Embarrassing. Better hand Bentley over to me. I can look him in the face and talk to him as man to man. You can have Johnny.

LORD SUMMERHAYS. Thank you. Ive lived so long in a country where a man may have fifty sons, who are no more to him than a regiment of soldiers, that I'm afraid Ive lost the English feeling about it.

TARLETON. [restless again] You mean Jinghiskahn. Ah yes. Good thing the empire. Educates us. Opens our minds. Knocks the Bible out of us. And civilizes the other chaps.

LORD SUMMERHAYS. Yes: it civilizes them. And it uncivilizes us. Their gain. Our loss, Tarleton, believe me, our loss.

TARLETON. Well, why not? Averages out the human race. Makes the nigger half an Englishman. Makes the Englishman half a nigger. LORD SUMMERHAYS. Speaking as the unfortunate Englishman in question, I dont like the process. If I had my life to live over again, I'd stay at home and supercivilize myself.

TARLETON. Nonsense! dont be selfish. Think how youve improved the other chaps. Look at the Spanish empire! Bad job for Spain, but splendid for South America. Look at what the Romans did for Britain! They burst up and had to clear out; but think of all they taught us! They were the making of us: I believe there was a Roman camp on Hindhead: I'll shew it to you tomorrow. Thats the good side of Imperialism: it's unselfish. I despise the Little Englanders: theyre always thinking about England. Smallminded. I'm for the Parliament of man, the federation of the world. Read Tennyson. [He settles down again]. Then theres the great food question.

LORD SUMMERHAYS. [apprehensively] Need we go into that this afternoon?

TARLETON. No; but I wish youd tell the Chickabiddy that the Jinghiskahns eat no end of toasted cheese, and that it's the secret of their amazing health and long life!

LORD SUMMERHAYS. Unfortunately they are neither healthy nor long lived. And they dont eat toasted cheese.

TARLETON. There you are! They would be if they ate it. Anyhow, say what you like, provided the moral is a Welsh rabbit for my supper.

LORD SUMMERHAYS. British morality in a nutshell!

TARLETON. [hugely amused] Yes. Ha ha! Awful hypocrites, aint we? They are interrupted by excited cries from the grounds.

HYPATIA. | Papa! Mamma! Come out as fast as you can. | Quick. Quick. |

BENTLEY. | Hello, governor! Come out. An aeroplane. | Look, look.

TARLETON. [starting up] Aeroplane! Did he say an aeroplane?

LORD SUMMERHAYS. Aeroplane! [A shadow falls on the pavilion; and some of the glass at the top is shattered and falls on the floor]. Tarleton and Lord Summerhays rush out through the pavilion into the garden.

HYPATIA. | Take care. Take care of the chimney. |

BENTLEY. | Come this side: it's coming right | where youre standing. |

TARLETON. | Hallo! where the devil are you | coming? youll have my roof off. |

LORD SUMMERHAYS| He's lost control.

MRS TARLETON. Look, look, Hypatia. There are two people in it.

BENTLEY. Theyve cleared it. Well steered!

TARLETON. | Yes; but theyre coming slam into the greenhouse. |

LORD SUMMERHAYS| Look out for the glass. |

MRS TARLETON. | Theyll break all the glass. Theyll | spoil all the grapes. |

BENTLEY. | Mind where youre coming. He'll | save it. No: theyre down. An appalling crash of breaking glass is heard. Everybody shrieks.

MRS TARLETON. | Oh, are they killed? John: are they killed? |

LORD SUMMERHAYS| Are you hurt? Is anything broken? Can you stand? |

HYPATIA. | Oh, you must be hurt. Are you sure? Shall I get | you some water? Or some wine? |

TARLETON. | Are you all right? Sure you wont have some | brandy just to take off the shock. THE AVIATOR. No, thank you. Quite right. Not a scratch. I assure you I'm all right.

BENTLEY. What luck! And what a smash! You are a lucky chap, I can tell you. The Aviator and Tarleton come in through the pavilion, followed by Lord Summerhays and Bentley, the Aviator on Tarleton's right. Bentley passes the Aviator and turns to have an admiring look at him. Lord Summerhays overtakes Tarleton less pointedly on the opposite side with the same object. THE AVIATOR. I'm really very sorry. I'm afraid Ive knocked your vinery into a cocked hat. (Effusively) You dont mind, do you?

TARLETON. Not a bit. Come in and have some tea. Stay to dinner. Stay over the week-end. All my life Ive wanted to fly. THE AVIATOR. [taking off his goggles] Youre really more than kind.

BENTLEY. Why, its Joey Percival.

PERCIVAL. Hallo, Ben! That you?

TARLETON. What! The man with three fathers!

PERCIVAL. Oh! has Ben been talking about me?

TARLETON. Consider yourself as one of the family—if you will do me the honor. And your friend too. Wheres your friend?

PERCIVAL. Oh, by the way! before he comes in: let me explain. I dont know him.

TARLETON. Eh?

PERCIVAL. Havnt even looked at him. I'm trying to make a club record with a passenger. The club supplied the passenger. He just got in; and Ive been too busy handling the aeroplane to look at him. I havnt said a word to him; and I cant answer for him socially; but hes an ideal passenger for a flyer. He saved me from a smash.

LORD SUMMERHAYS. I saw it. It was extraordinary. When you were thrown out he held on to the top bar with one hand. You came past him in the air, going straight for the glass. He caught you and turned you off into the flower bed, and then lighted beside you like a bird.

PERCIVAL. How he kept his head I cant imagine. Frankly, I didnt. The Passenger, also begoggled, comes in through the pavilion with Johnny and the two ladies. The Passenger comes between Percival and Tarleton, Mrs Tarleton between Lord Summerhays and her husband, Hypatia between Percival and Bentley, and Johnny to Bentley's right.

TARLETON. Just discussing your prowess, my dear sir. Magnificent. Youll stay to dinner. Youll stay the night. Stay over the week. The Chickabiddy will be delighted.

MRS TARLETON. Wont you take off your goggles and have some tea? The Passenger begins to remove the goggles.

TARLETON. Do. Have a wash. Johnny: take the gentleman to your room: I'll look after Mr Percival. They must— By this time the passenger has got the goggles off, and stands revealed as a remarkably good-looking woman.

MRS TARLETON. | Well I never!!! | | |

BENTLEY. | [in a whisper] Oh, I say! | | |

JOHNNY. | By George! | | |
All

LORD SUMMERHAYS| A lady! | to- |
| gether.

HYPATIA. | A woman! | | |

TARLETON. | [to Percival] You never told me— | |
|

PERCIVAL. | I hadnt the least idea— | An embarrassed pause.

PERCIVAL. I assure you if I'd had the faintest notion that my passenger was a lady I shouldnt have left you to shift for yourself in that selfish way.

LORD SUMMERHAYS. The lady seems to have shifted for both very effectually, sir.

PERCIVAL. Saved my life. I admit it most gratefully.

TARLETON. I must apologize, madam, for having offered you the civilities appropriate to the opposite sex. And yet, why opposite? We are all human: males and females of the same species. When the dress is the same the distinction vanishes. I'm proud to receive in my house a lady of evident refinement and distinction. Allow me to introduce myself: Tarleton: John Tarleton (seeing conjecture in the passenger's eye)—yes, yes: Tarleton's Underwear. My wife, Mrs Tarleton: youll excuse me for having in what I had taken to be a confidence between man and man alluded to her as the Chickabiddy. My daughter Hypatia, who has always wanted some adventure to drop out of the sky, and is now, I hope, satisfied at last. Lord Summerhays: a man known wherever the British flag waves. His son Bentley, engaged to Hypatia. Mr Joseph Percival, the promising son of three highly intellectual fathers.

HYPATIA. [startled] Bentley's friend? [Bentley nods].

TARLETON. [continuing, to the passenger] May I now ask to be allowed the pleasure of knowing your name? THE PASSENGER. My name is Lina Szczepanowska [pronouncing it Sh-Chepanovska].

PERCIVAL. Sh— I beg your pardon?

LINA. Szczepanowska.

PERCIVAL. [dubiously] Thank you.

TARLETON. [very politely] Would you mind saying it again?

LINA. Say fish.

TARLETON. Fish.

LINA. Say church.

TARLETON. Church.

LINA. Say fish church.

TARLETON. [remonstrating] But it's not good sense.

LINA. [inexorable] Say fish church.

TARLETON. Fish church.

LINA. Again.

TARLETON. No, but—[resigning himself] fish church.

LINA. Now say Szczepanowska.

TARLETON. Szczepanowska. Got it, by Gad. [A sibilant whispering becomes audible: they are all saying Sh-ch to themselves]. Szczepanowska! Not an English name, is it?

LINA. Polish. I'm a Pole.

TARLETON. Ah yes. Interesting nation. Lucky people to get the government of their country taken off their hands. Nothing to do but cultivate themselves. Same as we took Gibraltar off the hands of the Spaniards. Saves the Spanish taxpayer. Jolly good thing for us if the Germans took Portsmouth. Sit down, wont you? The group breaks up. Johnny and Bentley hurry to the pavilion and fetch the two wicker chairs. Johnny gives his to Lina. Hypatia and Percival take the chairs at the worktable. Lord Summerhays gives the chair at the vestibule end of the writing table to Mrs Tarleton; and Bentley replaces it with a wicker chair, which Lord Summerhays takes. Johnny remains standing behind the worktable, Bentley behind his father.

MRS TARLETON. [to Lina] Have some tea now, wont you?

LINA. I never drink tea.

TARLETON. [sitting down at the end of the writing table nearest Lina] Bad thing to aeroplane on, I should imagine. Too jumpy. Been up much?

LINA. Not in an aeroplane. Ive parachuted; but thats child's play.

MRS TARLETON. But arnt you very foolish to run such a dreadful risk?

LINA. You cant live without running risks.

MRS TARLETON. Oh, what a thing to say! Didnt you know you might have been killed?

LINA. That was why I went up.

HYPATIA. Of course. Cant you understand the fascination of the thing? the novelty! the daring! the sense of something happening!

LINA. Oh no. It's too tame a business for that. I went up for family reasons.

TARLETON. Eh? What? Family reasons?

MRS TARLETON. I hope it wasnt to spite your mother?

PERCIVAL. [quickly] Or your husband?

LINA. I'm not married. And why should I want to spite my mother?

HYPATIA. [aside to Percival] That was clever of you, Mr Percival.

PERCIVAL. What?

HYPATIA. To find out.

TARLETON. I'm in a difficulty. I cant understand a lady going up in an aeroplane for family reasons. It's rude to be curious and ask questions; but then it's inhuman to be indifferent, as if you didnt care.

LINA. I'll tell you with pleasure. For the last hundred and fifty years, not a single day has passed without some member of my family risking his life—or her life. It's a point of honor with us to keep up that tradition.

Usually several of us do it; but it happens that just at this moment it is being kept up by one of my brothers only. Early this morning I got a telegram from him to say that there had been a fire, and that he could do nothing for the rest of the week. Fortunately I had an invitation from the Aerial League to see this gentleman try to break the passenger record. I appealed to the President of the League to let me save the honor of my family. He arranged it for me.

TARLETON. Oh, I must be dreaming. This is stark raving nonsense.

LINA. [quietly] You are quite awake, sir.

JOHNNY. We cant all be dreaming the same thing, Governor.

TARLETON. Of course not, you duffer; but then I'm dreaming you as well as the lady.

MRS TARLETON. Dont be silly, John. The lady is only joking, I'm sure. [To Lina] I suppose your luggage is in the aeroplane.

PERCIVAL. Luggage was out of the question. If I stay to dinner I'm afraid I cant change unless youll lend me some clothes.

MRS TARLETON. Do you mean neither of you?

PERCIVAL. I'm afraid so.

MRS TARLETON. Oh well, never mind: Hypatia will lend the lady a gown.

LINA. Thank you: I'm quite comfortable as I am. I am not accustomed to gowns: they hamper me and make me feel ridiculous; so if you dont mind I shall not change.

MRS TARLETON. Well, I'm beginning to think I'm doing a bit of dreaming myself.

HYPATIA. [impatiently] Oh, it's all right, mamma. Johnny: look after Mr. Percival. [To Lina, rising] Come with me. Lina follows her to the inner door. They all rise.

JOHNNY. [to Percival] I'll shew you.

PERCIVAL. Thank you. Lina goes out with Hypatia, and Percival with Johnny.

MRS TARLETON. Well, this is a nice thing to happen! And look at the greenhouse! Itll cost thirty pounds to mend it. People have no right to do such things. And you invited them to dinner too! What sort of woman is that to have in our house when you know that all Hindhead will be calling on us to see that aeroplane? Bunny: come with me and help me to get all the people out of the grounds: I declare they came running as if theyd sprung up out of the earth [she makes for the inner door].

TARLETON. No: dont you trouble, Chickabiddy: I'll tackle em.

MRS TARLETON. Indeed youll do nothing of the kind: youll stay here quietly with Lord Summerhays. Youd invite them all to dinner. Come, Bunny. [She goes out, followed by Bentley. Lord Summerhays sits down again].

TARLETON. Singularly beautiful woman Summerhays. What do you make of her? She must be a princess. Whats this family of warriors and statesmen that risk their lives every day?

LORD SUMMERHAYS. They are evidently not warriors and statesmen, or they wouldnt do that.

TARLETON. Well, then, who the devil are they?

LORD SUMMERHAYS. I think I know. The last time I saw that lady, she did something I should not have thought possible.

TARLETON. What was that?

LORD SUMMERHAYS. Well, she walked backwards along a taut wire without a balancing pole and turned a somersault in the middle. I remember that her name was Lina, and that the other name was foreign; though I dont recollect it.

TARLETON. Szcz! You couldnt have forgotten that if youd heard it.

LORD SUMMERHAYS. I didnt hear it: I only saw it on a program. But it's clear shes an acrobat. It explains how she saved Percival. And it accounts for her family pride.

TARLETON. An acrobat, eh? Good, good, good! Summerhays: that brings her within reach. Thats better than a princess. I steeled this evergreen heart of mine when I thought she was a princess. Now I shall let it be touched. She is accessible. Good.

LORD SUMMERHAYS. I hope you are not serious. Remember: you have a family. You have a position. You are not in your first youth.

TARLETON. No matter. Theres magic in the night When the heart is young. My heart is young. Besides, I'm a married man, not a widower like you. A married man can do anything he likes if his wife dont mind. A widower cant be too careful. Not that I would have you think me an unprincipled man or a bad husband. I'm not. But Ive a superabundance of vitality. Read Pepys' Diary.

LORD SUMMERHAYS. The woman is your guest, Tarleton.

TARLETON. Well, is she? A woman I bring into my house is my guest. A woman you bring into my house is my guest. But a woman who drops bang down out of the sky into my greenhouse and smashes every blessed pane of glass in it must take her chance.

LORD SUMMERHAYS. Still, you know that my name must not be associated with any scandal. Youll be careful, wont you?

TARLETON. Oh Lord, yes. Yes, yes, yes, yes, yes. I was only joking, of course. Mrs Tarleton comes back through the inner door.

MRS TARLETON. Well I never! John: I dont think that young woman's right in her head. Do you know what shes just asked for?

TARLETON. Champagne?

MRS TARLETON. No. She wants a Bible and six oranges.

TARLETON. What?

MRS TARLETON. A Bible and six oranges.

TARLETON. I understand the oranges: shes doing an orange cure of some sort. But what on earth does she want the Bible for?

MRS TARLETON. I'm sure I cant imagine. She cant be right in her head.

LORD SUMMERHAYS. Perhaps she wants to read it.

MRS TARLETON. But why should she, on a weekday, at all events. What would you advise me to do, Lord Summerhays?

LORD SUMMERHAYS. Well, is there a Bible in the house?

TARLETON. Stacks of em. Theres the family Bible, and the Dore Bible, and the parallel revised version Bible, and the Doves Press Bible, and Johnny's Bible and Bobby's Bible and Patsy's Bible, and the Chickabiddy's Bible and my Bible; and I daresay the servants could raise a few more between them. Let her have the lot.

MRS TARLETON. Dont talk like that before Lord Summerhays, John.

LORD SUMMERHAYS. It doesnt matter, Mrs Tarleton: in Jinghiskahn it was a punishable offence to expose a Bible for sale. The empire has no religion. Lina comes in. She has left her cap in Hypatia's room. She stops on the landing just inside the door, and speaks over the handrail.

LINA. Oh, Mrs Tarleton, shall I be making myself very troublesome if I ask for a music-stand in my room as well?

TARLETON. Not at all. You can have the piano if you like. Or the gramophone. Have the gramophone.

LINA. No, thank you: no music.

MRS TARLETON. [going to the steps] Do you think it's good for you to eat so many oranges? Arnt you afraid of getting jaundice?

LINA. [coming down] Not in the least. But billiard balls will do quite as well.

MRS TARLETON. But you cant eat billiard balls, child!

TARLETON. Get em, Chickabiddy. I understand. [He imitates a juggler tossing up balls]. Eh?

LINA. [going to him, past his wife] Just so.

TARLETON. Billiard balls and cues. Plates, knives, and forks. Two paraffin lamps and a hatstand.

LINA. No: that is popular low-class business. In our family we touch nothing but classical work. Anybody can do lamps and hatstands. I can do silver bullets. That is really hard. [She passes on to Lord Summerhays, and looks gravely down at him as he sits by the writing table].

MRS TARLETON. Well, I'm sure I dont know what youre talking about; and I only hope you know yourselves. However, you shall have what you want, of course. [She goes up the steps and leaves the room].

LORD SUMMERHAYS. Will you forgive my curiosity? What is the Bible for?

LINA. To quiet my soul.

LORD SUMMERHAYS [with a sigh] Ah yes, yes. It no longer quiets mine, I am sorry to say.

LINA. That is because you do not know how to read it. Put it up before you on a stand; and open it at the Psalms. When you can read them and understand them, quite quietly and happily, and keep six balls in the air all the time, you are in perfect condition; and youll never make a mistake that evening. If you find you cant do that, then go and pray until you can. And be very careful that evening.

LORD SUMMERHAYS. Is that the usual form of test in your profession?

LINA. Nothing that we Szczepanowskis do is usual, my lord.

LORD SUMMERHAYS. Are you all so wonderful?

LINA. It is our profession to be wonderful.

LORD SUMMERHAYS. Do you never condescend to do as common people do? For instance, do you not pray as common people pray?

LINA. Common people do not pray, my lord: they only beg.

LORD SUMMERHAYS. You never ask for anything?

LINA. No.

LORD SUMMERHAYS. Then why do you pray?

LINA. To remind myself that I have a soul.

TARLETON. [walking about] True. Fine. Good. Beautiful. All this damned materialism: what good is it to anybody? Ive got a soul: dont tell me I havnt. Cut me up and you cant find it. Cut up a steam engine and you cant find the steam. But, by George, it makes the engine go. Say what you will, Summerhays, the divine spark is a fact.

LORD SUMMERHAYS. Have I denied it?

TARLETON. Our whole civilization is a denial of it. Read Walt Whitman.

LORD SUMMERHAYS. I shall go to the billiard room and get the balls for you.

LINA. Thank you. Lord Summerhays goes out through the vestibule door.

TARLETON. [going to her] Listen to me. [She turns quickly]. What you said just now was beautiful. You touch chords. You appeal to the poetry in a man. You inspire him. Come now! Youre a woman of the world: youre independent: you must have driven lots of men crazy. You know the sort of man I am, dont you? See through me at a glance, eh?

LINA. Yes. [She sits down quietly in the chair Lord Summerhays has just left].

TARLETON. Good. Well, do you like me? Dont misunderstand me: I'm perfectly aware that youre not going to fall in love at first sight with a ridiculous old shopkeeper. I cant help that ridiculous old shopkeeper. I have to carry him about with me whether I like it or not. I have to pay for his clothes, though I hate the cut of them: especially the waistcoat. I have to look at him in the glass while I'm shaving. I loathe him because hes a living lie. My soul's not like that: it's like yours. I want to make a fool of myself. About you. Will you let me?

LINA. [very calm] How much will you pay?

TARLETON. Nothing. But I'll throw as many sovereigns as you like into the sea to shew you that I'm in earnest.

LINA. Are those your usual terms?

TARLETON. No. I never made that bid before.

LINA. [producing a dainty little book and preparing to write in it] What did you say your name was?

TARLETON. John Tarleton. The great John Tarleton of Tarleton's Underwear.

LINA. [writing] T-a-r-l-e-t-o-n. Er—? [She looks up at him inquiringly].

TARLETON. [promptly] Fifty-eight.

LINA. Thank you. I keep a list of all my offers. I like to know what I'm considered worth.

TARLETON. Let me look.

LINA. [offering the book to him] It's in Polish.

TARLETON. Thats no good. Is mine the lowest offer?

LINA. No: the highest.

TARLETON. What do most of them come to? Diamonds? Motor cars? Furs? Villa at Monte Carlo?

LINA. Oh yes: all that. And sometimes the devotion of a lifetime.

TARLETON. Fancy that! A young man offering a woman his old age as a temptation!

LINA. By the way, you did not say how long.

TARLETON. Until you get tired of me.

LINA. Or until you get tired of me?

TARLETON. I never get tired. I never go on long enough for that. But when it becomes so grand, so inspiring that I feel that everything must be an anti-climax after that, then I run away.

LINA. Does she let you go without a struggle?

TARLETON. Yes. Glad to get rid of me. When love takes a man as it takes me—when it makes him great—it frightens a woman.

LINA. The lady here is your wife, isnt she? Dont you care for her?

TARLETON. Yes. And mind! she comes first always. I reserve her dignity even when I sacrifice my own. Youll respect that point of honor, wont you?

LINA. Only a point of honor?

TARLETON. [impulsively] No, by God! a point of affection as well.

LINA. [smiling, pleased with him] Shake hands, old pal [she rises and offers him her hand frankly].

TARLETON. [giving his hand rather dolefully] Thanks. That means no, doesnt it?

LINA. It means something that will last longer than yes. I like you. I admit you to my friendship. What a pity you were not trained when you were young! Youd be young still.

TARLETON. I suppose, to an athlete like you, I'm pretty awful, eh?

LINA. Shocking.

TARLETON. Too much crumb. Wrinkles. Yellow patches that wont come off. Short wind. I know. I'm ashamed of myself. I could do nothing on the high rope.

LINA. Oh yes: I could put you in a wheelbarrow and run you along, two hundred feet up.

TARLETON. [shuddering] Ugh! Well, I'd do even that for you. Read The Master Builder.

LINA. Have you learnt everything from books?

TARLETON. Well, have you learnt everything from the flying trapeze?

LINA. On the flying trapeze there is often another woman; and her life is in your hands every night and your life in hers.

TARLETON. Lina: I'm going to make a fool of myself. I'm going to cry [he crumples into the nearest chair].

LINA. Pray instead: dont cry. Why should you cry? Youre not the first I've said no to.

TARLETON. If you had said yes, should I have been the first then?

LINA. What right have you to ask? Have I asked am I the first?

TARLETON. Youre right: a vulgar question. To a man like me, everybody is the first. Life renews itself.

LINA. The youngest child is the sweetest.

TARLETON. Dont probe too deep, Lina. It hurts.

LINA. You must get out of the habit of thinking that these things matter so much. It's linendraperish.

TARLETON. Youre quite right. Ive often said so. All the same, it does matter; for I want to cry. [He buries his face in his arms on the work-table and sobs].

LINA. [going to him] O la la! [She slaps him vigorously, but not unkindly, on the shoulder]. Courage, old pal, courage! Have you a gymnasium here?

TARLETON. Theres a trapeze and bars and things in the billiard room.

LINA. Come. You need a few exercises. I'll teach you how to stop crying. [She takes his arm and leads him off into the vestibule]. A young man, cheaply dressed and strange in manner, appears in the garden; steals to the pavilion door; and looks in. Seeing that there is nobody, he enters cautiously until he has come far enough to see into the hatstand corner. He draws a revolver, and examines it, apparently to make sure that it is loaded. Then his attention is caught by the Turkish bath. He looks down the lunette, and opens the panels.

HYPATIA. [calling in the garden] Mr Percival! Mr Percival! Where are you? The young man makes for the door, but sees Percival coming. He turns and bolts into the Turkish bath, which he closes upon himself just in time to escape being caught by Percival, who runs in through the pavilion, bareheaded. He also, it appears, is in search of a hiding-place; for he stops and turns between the two tables to take a survey of the room; then runs into the corner between the end of the sideboard and the wall. Hypatia, excited, mischievous, her eyes glowing, runs in, precisely on his trail; turns at the same spot; and discovers him just as he makes a dash for the pavilion door. She flies back and intercepts him.

HYPATIA. Aha! arnt you glad Ive caught you?

PERCIVAL. [illhumoredly turning away from her and coming towards the writing table] No I'm not. Confound it, what sort of girl are you? What sort of house is this? Must I throw all good manners to the winds?

HYPATIA. [following him] Do, do, do, do, do. This is the house of a respectable shopkeeper, enormously rich. This is the respectable shopkeeper's daughter, tired of good manners. [Slipping her left hand into his right] Come, handsome young man, and play with the respectable shopkeeper's daughter.

PERCIVAL. [withdrawing quickly from her touch] No, no: dont you know you mustnt go on like this with a perfect stranger?

HYPATIA. Dropped down from the sky. Dont you know that you must always go on like this when you get the chance? You must come to the top of the hill and chase me through the bracken. You may kiss me if you catch me.

PERCIVAL. I shall do nothing of the sort.

HYPATIA. Yes you will: you cant help yourself. Come along. [She seizes his sleeve]. Fool, fool: come along. Dont you want to?

PERCIVAL. No: certainly not. I should never be forgiven if I did it.

HYPATIA. Youll never forgive yourself if you dont.

PERCIVAL. Nonsense. Youre engaged to Ben. Ben's my friend. What do you take me for?

HYPATIA. Ben's old. Ben was born old. Theyre all old here, except you and me and the man-woman or woman-man or whatever you call her that came with you. They never do anything: they only discuss whether what other people do is right. Come and give them something to discuss.

PERCIVAL. I will do nothing incorrect.

HYPATIA. Oh, dont be afraid, little boy: youll get nothing but a kiss; and I'll fight like the devil to keep you from getting that. But we must play on the hill and race through the heather.

PERCIVAL. Why?

HYPATIA. Because we want to, handsome young man.

PERCIVAL. But if everybody went on in this way—

HYPATIA. How happy! oh how happy the world would be!

PERCIVAL. But the consequences may be serious.

HYPATIA. Nothing is worth doing unless the consequences may be serious. My father says so; and I'm my father's daughter.

PERCIVAL. I'm the son of three fathers. I mistrust these wild impulses.

HYPATIA. Take care. Youre letting the moment slip. I feel the first chill of the wave of prudence. Save me.

PERCIVAL. Really, Miss Tarleton [she strikes him across the face] —Damn you! [Recovering himself, horrified at his lapse] I beg your pardon; but since weve both forgotten ourselves, youll please allow me to leave the house. [He turns towards the inner door, having left his cap in the bedroom].

HYPATIA. [standing in his way] Are you ashamed of having said "Damn you" to me?

PERCIVAL. I had no right to say it. I'm very much ashamed of it. I have already begged your pardon.

HYPATIA. And youre not ashamed of having said "Really, Miss Tarleton."

PERCIVAL. Why should I?

HYPATIA. O man, man! mean, stupid, cowardly, selfish masculine male man! You ought to have been a governess. I was expelled from school for saying that the very next person that said "Really, Miss Tarleton," to me, I would strike her across the face. You were the next.

PERCIVAL. I had no intention of being offensive. Surely there is nothing that can wound any lady in—[He hesitates, not quite convinced]. At least—er—I really didnt mean to be disagreeable.

HYPATIA. Liar.

PERCIVAL. Of course if youre going to insult me, I am quite helpless. Youre a woman: you can say what you like.

HYPATIA. And you can only say what you dare. Poor wretch: it isnt much. [He bites his lip, and sits down, very much annoyed]. Really, Mr Percival! You sit down in the presence of a lady and leave her standing. [He rises hastily]. Ha, ha! Really, Mr Percival! Oh really, really, really, really, really, Mr Percival! How do you like it? Wouldnt you rather I damned you?

PERCIVAL. Miss Tarleton—

HYPATIA. [caressingly] Hypatia, Joey. Patsy, if you like.

PERCIVAL. Look here: this is no good. You want to do what you like?

HYPATIA. Dont you?

PERCIVAL. No. Ive been too well brought up. Ive argued all through this thing; and I tell you I'm not prepared to cast off the social bond. It's like a corset: it's a support to the figure even if it does squeeze and deform it a bit. I want to be free.

HYPATIA. Well, I'm tempting you to be free.

PERCIVAL. Not at all. Freedom, my good girl, means being able to count on how other people will behave. If every man who dislikes me is to throw a handful of mud in my face, and every woman who likes me is to behave like Potiphar's wife, then I shall be a slave: the slave of uncertainty: the slave of fear: the worst of all slaveries. How would you like it if every laborer you met in the road were to make love to you? No. Give me the blessed protection of a good stiff conventionality among thoroughly well-brought up ladies and gentlemen.

HYPATIA. Another talker! Men like conventions because men made them. I didnt make them: I dont like them: I wont keep them. Now, what will you do?

PERCIVAL. Bolt. [He runs out through the pavilion].

HYPATIA. I'll catch you. [She dashes off in pursuit]. During this conversation the head of the scandalized man in the Turkish bath has repeatedly risen from the lunette, with a strong expression of moral shock. It vanishes abruptly as the two turn towards it in their flight. At the same moment Tarleton comes back through the vestibule door, exhausted by severe and unaccustomed exercise.

TARLETON. [looking after the flying figures with amazement] Hallo, Patsy: whats up? Another aeroplane? [They are far too preoccupied to hear him; and he is left staring after them as they rush away through the garden. He goes to the pavilion door and looks up; but the heavens are empty. His exhaustion disables him from further inquiry. He dabs his brow with his handkerchief, and walks stiffly to the nearest convenient support, which happens to be the Turkish bath. He props himself upon it with his elbow, and covers his eyes with his hand for a moment. After a few sighing breaths, he feels a little better, and uncovers his eyes. The man's head rises from the lunette a few inches from his nose. He recoils from the bath with a violent start]. Oh Lord! My brain's gone. [Calling piteously] Chickabiddy! [He staggers down to the writing table].

THE MAN. [coming out of the bath, pistol in hand] Another sound; and youre a dead man.

TARLETON. [braced] Am I? Well, youre a live one: thats one comfort. I thought you were a ghost. [He sits down, quite undisturbed by the pistol] Who are you; and what the devil were you doing in my new Turkish bath?

THE MAN. [with tragic intensity] I am the son of Lucinda Titmus.

TARLETON. [the name conveying nothing to him] Indeed? And how is she? Quite well, I hope, eh?

THE MAN. She is dead. Dead, my God! and youre alive.

TARLETON. [unimpressed by the tragedy, but sympathetic] Oh! Lost your mother? Thats sad. I'm sorry. But we cant all have the luck to survive our mothers, and be nursed out of the world by the hands that nursed us into it.

THE MAN. Much you care, damn you!

TARLETON. Oh, dont cut up rough. Face it like a man. You see I didnt know your mother; but Ive no doubt she was an excellent woman.

THE MAN. Not know her! Do you dare to stand there by her open grave and deny that you knew her?

TARLETON. [trying to recollect] What did you say her name was?

THE MAN. Lucinda Titmus.

TARLETON. Well, I ought to remember a rum name like that if I ever heard it. But I dont. Have you a photograph or anything?

THE MAN. Forgotten even the name of your victim!

TARLETON. Oh! she was my victim, was she?

THE MAN. She was. And you shall see her face again before you die, dead as she is. I have a photograph.

TARLETON. Good.

THE MAN. Ive two photographs.

TARLETON. Still better. Treasure the mother's pictures. Good boy!

THE MAN. One of them as you knew her. The other as she became when you flung her aside, and she withered into an old woman.

TARLETON. She'd have done that anyhow, my lad. We all grow old. Look at me! [Seeing that the man is embarrassed by his pistol in fumbling for the photographs with his left hand in his breast pocket] Let me hold the gun for you.

THE MAN. [retreating to the worktable] Stand back. Do you take me for a fool?

TARLETON. Well, youre a little upset, naturally. It does you credit.

THE MAN. Look here, upon this picture and on this. [He holds out the two photographs like a hand at cards, and points to them with the pistol].

TARLETON. Good. Read Shakespear: he has a word for every occasion. [He takes the photographs, one in each hand, and looks from one to the other, pleased and interested, but without any sign of recognition] What a pretty girl! Very pretty. I can imagine myself falling in love with her when I was your age. I wasnt a bad-looking young fellow myself in those days. [Looking at the other] Curious that we should both have gone the same way.

THE MAN. You and she the same way! What do you mean?

TARLETON. Both got stout, I mean.

THE MAN. Would you have had her deny herself food?

TARLETON. No: it wouldnt have been any use. It's constitutional. No matter how little you eat you put on flesh if youre made that way. [He resumes his study of the earlier photograph].

THE MAN. Is that all the feeling that rises in you at the sight of the face you once knew so well?

TARLETON. [too much absorbed in the portrait to heed him] Funny that I cant remember! Let this be a lesson to you, young man. I could go into court tomorrow and swear I never saw that face before in my life if it wasnt for that brooch [pointing to the photograph]. Have you got that brooch, by the way? [The man again resorts to his breast pocket]. You seem to carry the whole family property in that pocket.

THE MAN. [producing a brooch] Here it is to prove my bona fides.

TARLETON. [pensively putting the photographs on the table and taking the brooch] I bought that brooch in Cheapside from a man with a yellow wig and a cast in his left eye. Ive never set eyes on him from that day to this. And yet I remember that man; and I cant remember your mother.

THE MAN. Monster! Without conscience! without even memory! You left her to her shame—

TARLETON. [throwing the brooch on the table and rising pepperily] Come, come, young man! none of that. Respect the romance of your mother's youth. Dont you start throwing stones at her. I dont recall her features just at this moment; but Ive no doubt she was kind to me and we were happy together. If you have a word to say against her, take yourself out of my house and say it elsewhere.

THE MAN. What sort of a joker are you? Are you trying to put me in the wrong, when you have to answer to me for a crime that would make every honest man spit at you as you passed in the street if I were to make it known?

TARLETON. You read a good deal, dont you?

THE MAN. What if I do? What has that to do with your infamy and my mother's doom?

TARLETON. There, you see! Doom! Thats not good sense; but it's literature. Now it happens that I'm a tremendous reader: always was. When I was your age I read books of that sort by the bushel: the Doom sort, you know. It's odd, isnt it, that you and I should be like one another in that respect? Can you account for it in any way?

THE MAN. No. What are you driving at?

TARLETON. Well, do you know who your father was?

THE MAN. I see what you mean now. You dare set up to be my father. Thank heaven Ive not a drop of your vile blood in my veins.

TARLETON. [sitting down again with a shrug] Well, if you wont be civil, theres no pleasure in talking to you, is there? What do you want? Money?

THE MAN. How dare you insult me?

TARLETON. Well, what do you want?

THE MAN. Justice.

TARLETON. Youre quite sure thats all?

THE MAN. It's enough for me.

TARLETON. A modest sort of demand, isnt it? Nobody ever had it since the world began, fortunately for themselves; but you must have it, must you? Well, youve come to the wrong shop for it: youll get no justice here: we dont keep it. Human nature is what we stock.

THE MAN. Human nature! Debauchery! gluttony! selfishness! robbery of the poor! Is that what you call human nature?

TARLETON. No: thats what you call it. Come, my lad! Whats the matter with you? You dont look starved; and youve a decent suit of clothes.

THE MAN. Forty-two shillings.

TARLETON. They can do you a very decent suit for forty-two shillings. Have you paid for it?

THE MAN. Do you take me for a thief? And do you suppose I can get credit like you?

TARLETON. Then you were able to lay your hand on forty-two shillings. Judging from your conversational style, I should think you must spend at least a shilling a week on romantic literature.

THE MAN. Where would I get a shilling a week to spend on books when I can hardly keep myself decent? I get books at the Free Library.

TARLETON [springing to his feet] What!!!

THE MAN. [recoiling before his vehemence] The Free Library. Theres no harm in that.

TARLETON. Ingrate! I supply you with free books; and the use you make of them is to persuade yourself that it's a fine thing to shoot me. [He throws himself doggedly back into his chair]. I'll never give another penny to a Free Library.

THE MAN. Youll never give another penny to anything. This is the end: for you and me.

TARLETON. Pooh! Come, come, man! talk business. Whats wrong? Are you out of employment?

THE MAN. No. This is my Saturday afternoon. Dont flatter yourself that I'm a loafer or a criminal. I'm a cashier; and I defy you to say that my cash has ever been a farthing wrong. Ive a right to call you to account because my hands are clean.

TARLETON. Well, call away. What have I to account for? Had you a hard time with your mother? Why didnt she ask me for money?

THE MAN. She'd have died first. Besides, who wanted your money? Do you suppose we lived in the gutter? My father maynt have been in as large a way as you; but he was better connected; and his shop was as respectable as yours.

TARLETON. I suppose your mother brought him a little capital.

THE MAN. I dont know. Whats that got to do with you?

TARLETON. Well, you say she and I knew one another and parted. She must have had something off me then, you know. One doesnt get out of these things for nothing. Hang it, young man: do you suppose Ive no heart? Of course she had her due; and she found a husband with it, and set him up in business with it, and brought you up respectably; so what the devil have you to complain of?

THE MAN. Are women to be ruined with impunity?

TARLETON. I havnt ruined any woman that I'm aware of. Ive been the making of you and your mother.

THE MAN. Oh, I'm a fool to listen to you and argue with you. I came here to kill you and then kill myself.

TARLETON. Begin with yourself, if you dont mind. Ive a good deal of business to do still before I die. Havnt you?

THE MAN. No. Thats just it: Ive no business to do. Do you know what my life is? I spend my days from nine to six—nine hours of daylight and fresh air—in a stuffy little den counting another man's money. Ive an intellect: a mind and a brain and a soul; and the use he makes of them is to fix them on his tuppences and his eighteenpences and his two pound seventeen and tenpences and see how much they come to at the end of the day and take care that no one steals them. I enter and enter, and add and add, and take money and give change, and fill cheques and stamp receipts; and not a penny of that money is my own: not one of those transactions has the smallest interest for me or anyone else in the world but him; and even he couldnt stand it if he had to do it all himself. And I'm envied: aye, envied for the variety and liveliness of my job, by the poor devil of a bookkeeper that has to copy all my entries over again. Fifty thousand entries a year that poor wretch makes; and not ten out of the fifty thousand ever has to be referred to again; and when all the figures are counted up and the balance sheet made out, the boss isnt a penny the richer than he'd be if bookkeeping had never been invented. Of all the damnable waste of human life that ever was invented, clerking is the very worst.

TARLETON. Why not join the territorials?

THE MAN. Because I shouldnt be let. He hasnt even the sense to see that it would pay him to get some cheap soldiering out of me. How can a man tied to a desk from nine to six be anything—be even a man, let alone a soldier? But I'll teach him and you a lesson. Ive had enough of living a dog's life and despising myself for it. Ive had enough of being talked down to by hogs like you, and wearing my life out for a salary that wouldnt keep you in cigars. Youll never believe that a clerk's a man until one of us makes an example of one of you.

TARLETON. Despotism tempered by assassination, eh?

THE MAN. Yes. Thats what they do in Russia. Well, a business office is Russia as far as the clerks are concerned. So dont you take it so coolly. You think I'm not going to do it; but I am.

TARLETON. [rising and facing him] Come, now, as man to man! It's not my fault that youre poorer than I am; and it's not your fault that I'm richer than you. And if you could undo all that passed between me and your mother, you wouldnt undo it; and neither would she. But youre sick of your slavery; and you want to be the hero of a romance and to get into the papers. Eh? A son revenges his mother's shame. Villain weltering in his gore. Mother: look down from heaven and receive your unhappy son's last sigh.

THE MAN. Oh, rot! do you think I read novelettes? And do you suppose I believe such superstitions as heaven? I go to church because the boss told me I'd get the sack if I didnt. Free England! Ha! [Lina appears at the pavilion door, and comes swiftly and noiselessly forward on seeing the man with a pistol in his hand].

TARLETON. Youre afraid of getting the sack; but youre not afraid to shoot yourself.

THE MAN. Damn you! youre trying to keep me talking until somebody comes. [He raises the pistol desperately, but not very resolutely].

LINA. [at his right elbow] Somebody has come.

THE MAN [turning on her] Stand off. I'll shoot you if you lay a hand on me. I will, by God.

LINA. You cant cover me with that pistol. Try. He tries, presenting the pistol at her face. She moves round him in the opposite direction to the hands of a clock with a light dancing step. He finds it impossible to cover her with the pistol: she is always too far to his left. Tarleton, behind him, grips his wrist and drags his arm straight up, so that the pistol points to the ceiling. As he tries to turn on his assailant, Lina grips his other wrist.

LINA. Please stop. I cant bear to twist anyone's wrist; but I must if you dont let the pistol go.

THE MAN. [letting Tarleton take it from him] All right: I'm done. Couldnt even do that job decently. Thats a clerk all over. Very well: send for your damned police and make an end of it. I'm accustomed to prison from nine to six: I daresay I can stand it from six to nine as well.

TARLETON. Dont swear. Thats a lady. [He throws the pistol on the writing table].

THE MAN. [looking at Lina in amazement] Beaten by a female! It needed only this. [He collapses in the chair near the worktable, and hides his face. They cannot help pitying him].

LINA. Old pal: dont call the police. Lend him a bicycle and let him get away.

THE MAN. I cant ride a bicycle. I never could afford one. I'm not even that much good.

TARLETON. If I gave you a hundred pound note now to go and have a good spree with, I wonder would you know how to set about it. Do you ever take a holiday?

THE MAN. Take! I got four days last August.

TARLETON. What did you do?

THE MAN. I did a cheap trip to Folkestone. I spent sevenpence on dropping pennies into silly automatic machines and peepshows of rowdy girls having a jolly time. I spent a penny on the lift and fourpence on refreshments. That cleaned me out. The rest of the time I was so miserable that I was glad to get back to the office. Now you know.

LINA. Come to the gymnasium: I'll teach you how to make a man of yourself. [The man is about to rise irresolutely, from the mere habit of doing what he is told, when Tarleton stops him].

TARLETON. Young man: dont. Youve tried to shoot me; but I'm not vindictive. I draw the line at putting a man on the rack. If you want every joint in your body stretched until it's an agony to live—until you have an unnatural feeling that all your muscles are singing and laughing with pain—then go to the gymnasium with that lady. But youll be more comfortable in jail.

LINA. [greatly amused] Was that why you went away, old pal? Was that the telegram you said you had forgotten to send? Mrs Tarleton comes in hastily through the inner door.

MRS TARLETON. [on the steps] Is anything the matter, John? Nurse says she heard you calling me a quarter of an hour ago; and that your voice sounded as if you were ill. [She comes between Tarleton and the man.] Is anything the matter?

TARLETON. This is the son of an old friend of mine. Mr—er—Mr Gunner. [To the man, who rises awkwardly]. My wife.

MRS TARLETON. Good evening to you.

GUNNER. Er— [He is too nervous to speak, and makes a shambling bow]. Bentley looks in at the pavilion door, very peevish, and too preoccupied with his own affairs to pay any attention to those of the company.

BENTLEY. I say: has anybody seen Hypatia? She promised to come out with me; and I cant find her anywhere. And wheres Joey?

GUNNER. [suddenly breaking out aggressively, being incapable of any middle way between submissiveness and violence] I can tell you where Hypatia is. I can tell you where Joey is. And I say it's a scandal and an infamy. If people only knew what goes on in this so-called respectable house it would be put a stop to. These are the morals of our pious capitalist class! This is your rotten bourgeoisie! This!—

MRS TARLETON. Dont you dare use such language in company. I wont allow it.

TARLETON. All right, Chickabiddy: it's not bad language: it's only Socialism.

MRS TARLETON. Well, I wont have any Socialism in my house.

TARLETON. [to Gunner] You hear what Mrs Tarleton says. Well, in this house everybody does what she says or out they go.

GUNNER. Do you suppose I want to stay? Do you think I would breathe this polluted atmosphere a moment longer than I could help?

BENTLEY. [running forward between Lina and Gunner] But what did you mean by what you said about Miss Tarleton and Mr Percival, you beastly rotter, you?

GUNNER. [to Tarleton] Oh! is Hypatia your daughter? And Joey is Mister Percival, is he? One of your set, I suppose. One of the smart set! One of the bridge-playing, eighty-horse-power, week-ender set! One of the johnnies I slave for! Well, Joey has more decency than your daughter, anyhow. The women are the worst. I never believed it til I saw it with my own eyes. Well, it wont last for ever. The writing is on the wall. Rome fell. Babylon fell. Hindhead's turn will come.

MRS TARLETON. [naively looking at the wall for the writing] Whatever are you talking about, young man?

GUNNER. I know what I'm talking about. I went into that Turkish bath a boy: I came out a man.

MRS TARLETON. Good gracious! hes mad. [To Lina] Did John make him take a Turkish bath?

LINA. No. He doesnt need Turkish baths: he needs to put on a little flesh. I dont understand what it's all about. I found him trying to shoot Mr Tarleton.

MRS TARLETON. [with a scream] Oh! and John encouraging him, I'll be bound! Bunny: you go for the police. [To Gunner] I'll teach you to come into my house and shoot my husband.

GUNNER. Teach away. I never asked to be let off. I'm ashamed to be free instead of taking my part with the rest. Women—beautiful women of noble birth—are going to prison for their opinions. Girl students in Russia go to the gallows; let themselves be cut in pieces with the knout, or driven through the frozen snows of Siberia, sooner than stand looking on tamely at the world being made a hell for the toiling millions. If you were not all skunks and cowards youd be suffering with them instead of battening here on the plunder of the poor.

MRS TARLETON. [much vexed] Oh, did you ever hear such silly nonsense? Bunny: go and tell the gardener to send over one of his men to Grayshott for the police.

GUNNER. I'll go with him. I intend to give myself up. I'm going to expose what Ive seen here, no matter what the consequences may be to my miserable self.

TARLETON. Stop. You stay where you are, Ben. Chickabiddy: youve never had the police in. If you had, youd not be in a hurry to have them in again. Now, young man: cut the cackle; and tell us, as short as you can, what did you see?

GUNNER. I cant tell you in the presence of ladies.

MRS TARLETON. Oh, you are tiresome. As if it mattered to anyone what you saw. Me! A married woman that might be your mother. [To Lina] And I'm sure youre not particular, if youll excuse my saying so.

TARLETON. Out with it. What did you see?

GUNNER. I saw your daughter with my own eyes—oh well, never mind what I saw.

BENTLEY. [almost crying with anxiety] You beastly rotter, I'll get Joey to give you such a hiding—

TARLETON. You cant leave it at that, you know. What did you see my daughter doing?

GUNNER. After all, why shouldnt she do it? The Russian students do it. Women should be as free as men. I'm a fool. I'm so full of your bourgeois morality that I let myself be shocked by the application of my own revolutionary principles. If she likes the man why shouldnt she tell him so?

MRS TARLETON. I do wonder at you, John, letting him talk like this before everybody. [Turning rather tartly to Lina] Would you mind going away to the drawing-room just for a few minutes, Miss Chipenoska. This is a private family matter, if you dont mind.

LINA. I should have gone before, Mrs Tarleton, if there had been anyone to protect Mr Tarleton and the young gentleman.

TARLETON. Youre quite right, Miss Lina: you must stand by. I could have tackled him this morning; but since you put me through those exercises I'd rather die than even shake hands with a man, much less fight him.

GUNNER. It's all of a piece here. The men effeminate, the women unsexed—

TARLETON. Dont begin again, old chap. Keep it for Trafalgar Square. HYPATIA'S VOICE OUTSIDE. No, no. [She breaks off in a stifled half laugh, half scream, and is seen darting across the garden with Percival in hot pursuit. Immediately afterwards she appears again, and runs into the pavilion. Finding it full of people, including a stranger, she stops; but Percival, flushed and reckless, rushes in and seizes her before he, too, realizes that they are not alone. He releases her in confusion]. Dead silence. They are all afraid to look at one another except Mrs Tarleton, who stares sternly at Hypatia. Hypatia is the first to recover her presence of mind.

HYPATIA. Excuse me rushing in like this. Mr Percival has been chasing me down the hill.

GUNNER. Who chased him up it? Dont be ashamed. Be fearless. Be truthful.

TARLETON. Gunner: will you go to Paris for a fortnight? I'll pay your expenses.

HYPATIA. What do you mean?

GUNNER. There was a silent witness in the Turkish bath.

TARLETON. I found him hiding there. Whatever went on here, he saw and heard. Thats what he means.

PERCIVAL. [sternly approaching Gunner, and speaking with deep but contained indignation] Am I to understand you as daring to put forward the monstrous and blackguardly lie that this lady behaved improperly in my presence?

GUNNER. [turning white] You know what I saw and heard. Hypatia, with a gleam of triumph in her eyes, slips noiselessly into the swing chair, and watches Percival and Gunner, swinging slightly, but otherwise motionless.

PERCIVAL. I hope it is not necessary for me to assure you all that there is not one word of truth—not one grain of substance—in this rascally calumny, which no man with a spark of decent feeling would have uttered even if he had been ignorant enough to believe it. Miss Tarleton's conduct, since I have had the honor of knowing her, has been, I need hardly say, in every respect beyond reproach. [To Gunner] As for you, sir, youll have the goodness to come out with me immediately. I have some business with you which cant be settled in Mrs Tarleton's presence or in her house.

GUNNER. [painfully frightened] Why should I go out with you?

PERCIVAL. Because I intend that you shall.

GUNNER. I wont be bullied by you. [Percival makes a threatening step towards him]. Police! [He tries to bolt; but Percival seizes him]. Leave me go, will you? What right have you to lay hands on me?

TARLETON. Let him run for it, Mr Percival. Hes very poor company. We shall be well rid of him. Let him go.

PERCIVAL. Not until he has taken back and made the fullest apology for the abominable lie he has told. He shall do that or he shall defend himself as best he can against the most thorough thrashing I'm capable of giving him. [Releasing Gunner, but facing him ominously] Take your choice. Which is it to be?

GUNNER. Give me a fair chance. Go and stick at a desk from nine to six for a month, and let me have your grub and your sport and your lessons in boxing, and I'll fight you fast enough. You know I'm no good or you darent bully me like this.

PERCIVAL. You should have thought of that before you attacked a lady with a dastardly slander. I'm waiting for your decision. I'm rather in a hurry, please.

GUNNER. I never said anything against the lady.

MRS TARLETON. | Oh, listen to that! |

BENTLEY. | What a liar! |

HYPATIA. | Oh! |

TARLETON. | Oh, come!

PERCIVAL. We'll have it in writing, if you dont mind. [Pointing to the writing table] Sit down; and take that pen in your hand. [Gunner looks irresolutely a little way round; then obeys]. Now write. "I," whatever your name is—

GUNNER [after a vain attempt] I cant. My hand's shaking too much. You see it's no use. I'm doing my best. I cant.

PERCIVAL. Mr Summerhays will write it: you can sign it.

BENTLEY. [insolently to Gunner] Get up. [Gunner obeys; and Bentley, shouldering him aside towards Percival, takes his place and prepares to write].

PERCIVAL. Whats your name?

GUNNER. John Brown.

TARLETON. Oh come! Couldnt you make it Horace Smith? or Algernon Robinson?

GUNNER. [agitatedly] But my name is John Brown. There are really John Browns. How can I help it if my name's a common one?

BENTLEY. Shew us a letter addressed to you.

GUNNER. How can I? I never get any letters: I'm only a clerk. I can shew you J. B. on my handkerchief. [He takes out a not very clean one].

BENTLEY. [with disgust] Oh, put it up again. Let it go at John Brown.

PERCIVAL. Where do you live?

GUNNER. 4 Chesterfield Parade, Kentish Town, N.W.

PERCIVAL. [dictating] I, John Brown, of 4 Chesterfield Parade, Kentish Town, do hereby voluntarily confess that on the 31st May 1909 I— [To Tarleton] What did he do exactly?

TARLETON. [dictating] —I trespassed on the land of John Tarleton at Hindhead, and effected an unlawful entry into his house, where I secreted myself in a portable Turkish bath—

BENTLEY. Go slow, old man. Just a moment. "Turkish bath"—yes?

TARLETON. [continuing] —with a pistol, with which I threatened to take the life of the said John Tarleton—

MRS TARLETON. Oh, John! You might have been killed.

TARLETON. —and was prevented from doing so only by the timely arrival of the celebrated Miss Lina Szczepanowska.

MRS TARLETON. Is she celebrated? [Apologetically] I never dreamt—

BENTLEY. Look here: I'm awfully sorry; but I cant spell Szczepanowska.

PERCIVAL. I think it's S, z, c, z— [Lina gives him her visiting-card]. Thank you. [He throws it on Bentley's blotter].

BENTLEY. Thanks awfully. [He writes the name].

TARLETON. [to Percival] Now it's your turn.

PERCIVAL. [dictating] I further confess that I was guilty of uttering an abominable calumny concerning Miss Hypatia Tarleton, for which there was not a shred of foundation. Impressive silence whilst Bentley writes.

BENTLEY. "foundation"?

PERCIVAL. I apologize most humbly to the lady and her family for my conduct— [he waits for Bentley to write].

BENTLEY. "conduct"?

PERCIVAL. —and I promise Mr Tarleton not to repeat it, and to amend my life—

BENTLEY. "amend my life"?

PERCIVAL. —and to do what in me lies to prove worthy of his kindness in giving me another chance—

BENTLEY. "another chance"?

PERCIVAL. —and refraining from delivering me up to the punishment I so richly deserve.

BENTLEY. "richly deserve."

PERCIVAL. [to Hypatia] Does that satisfy you, Miss Tarleton?

HYPATIA. Yes: that will teach him to tell lies next time.

BENTLEY. [rising to make place for Gunner and handing him the pen] You mean it will teach him to tell the truth next time.

TARLETON. Ahem! Do you, Patsy?

PERCIVAL. Be good enough to sign. [Gunner sits down helplessly and dips the pen in the ink]. I hope what you are signing is no mere form of words to you, and that you not only say you are sorry, but that you are sorry. Lord Summerhays and Johnny come in through the pavilion door.

MRS TARLETON. Stop. Mr Percival: I think, on Hypatia's account, Lord Summerhays ought to be told about this. Lord Summerhays, wondering what the matter is, comes forward between Percival and Lina. Johnny stops beside Hypatia.

PERCIVAL. Certainly.

TARLETON. [uneasily] Take my advice, and cut it short. Get rid of him.

MRS TARLETON. Hypatia ought to have her character cleared.

TARLETON. You let well alone, Chickabiddy. Most of our characters will bear a little careful dusting; but they wont bear scouring. Patsy is jolly well out of it. What does it matter, anyhow?

PERCIVAL. Mr Tarleton: we have already said either too much or not enough. Lord Summerhays: will you be kind enough to witness the declaration this man has just signed?

GUNNER. I havnt yet. Am I to sign now?

PERCIVAL. Of course. [Gunner, who is now incapable of doing anything on his own initiative, signs]. Now stand up and read your declaration to this gentleman. [Gunner makes a vague movement and looks stupidly round. Percival adds peremptorily] Now, please.

GUNNER [rising apprehensively and reading in a hardly audible voice, like a very sick man] I, John Brown, of 4 Chesterfield Parade, Kentish Town, do hereby voluntarily confess that on the 31st May 1909 I trespassed on the land of John Tarleton at Hindhead, and effected an unlawful entry into his house, where I secreted myself in a portable Turkish bath, with a pistol, with which I threatened to take the life of the said John Tarleton, and was prevented from doing so only by the timely arrival of the celebrated Miss Lena Sh-Sh-sheepanossika. I further confess that I was guilty of uttering an abominable calumny concerning Miss Hypatia Tarleton, for which there was not a shred of foundation. I apologize most humbly to the lady and her family for my conduct; and I promise Mr Tarleton not to repeat it, and to amend my life, and to do what in me lies to prove worthy of his kindness in giving me another chance and refraining from delivering me up to the punishment I so richly deserve. A short and painful silence follows. Then Percival speaks.

PERCIVAL. Do you consider that sufficient, Lord Summerhays?

LORD SUMMERHAYS. Oh quite, quite.

PERCIVAL. [to Hypatia] Lord Summerhays would probably like to hear you say that you are satisfied, Miss Tarleton.

HYPATIA. [coming out of the swing, and advancing between Percival and Lord Summerhays] I must say that you have behaved like a perfect gentleman, Mr. Percival.

PERCIVAL. [first bowing to Hypatia, and then turning with cold contempt to Gunner, who is standing helpless] We need not trouble you any further. [Gunner turns vaguely towards the pavilion].

JOHNNY [with less refined offensiveness, pointing to the pavilion] Thats your way. The gardener will shew you the shortest way into the road. Go the shortest way.

GUNNER. [oppressed and disconcerted, hardly knows how to get out of the room] Yes, sir. I— [He turns again, appealing to Tarleton] Maynt I have my mother's photographs back again? [Mrs Tarleton pricks up her ears].

TARLETON. Eh? What? Oh, the photographs! Yes, yes, yes: take them. [Gunner takes them from the table, and is creeping away, when Mrs Tarleton puts out her hand and stops him].

MRS TARLETON. Whats this, John? What were you doing with his mother's photographs?

TARLETON. Nothing, nothing. Never mind, Chickabiddy: it's all right.

MRS TARLETON. [snatching the photographs from Gunner's irresolute fingers, and recognizing them at a glance] Lucy Titmus! Oh John, John!

TARLETON. [grimly, to Gunner] Young man: youre a fool; but youve just put the lid on this job in a masterly manner. I knew you would. I told you all to let well alone. You wouldnt; and now you must take the consequences—or rather I must take them.

MRS TARLETON. [to Gunner] Are you Lucy's son?

GUNNER. Yes.

MRS TARLETON. And why didnt you come to me? I didnt turn my back on your mother when she came to me in her trouble. Didnt you know that?

GUNNER. No. She never talked to me about anything.

TARLETON. How could she talk to her own son? Shy, Summerhays, shy. Parent and child. Shy. [He sits down at the end of the writing table nearest the sideboard like a man resigned to anything that fate may have in store for him].

MRS TARLETON. Then how did you find out?

GUNNER. From her papers after she died.

MRS TARLETON. [shocked] Is Lucy dead? And I never knew! [With an effusion of tenderness] And you here being treated like that, poor orphan, with nobody to take your part! Tear up that foolish paper, child;

and sit down and make friends with me.

JOHNNY. | Hallo, mother this is all very well, you know— |

PERCIVAL. | But may I point out, Mrs Tarleton, that— |

BENTLEY. | Do you mean that after what he said of— |

HYPATIA. | Oh, look here, mamma: this is really—

MRS TARLETON. Will you please speak one at a time? Silence. PERCIVAL [in a very gentlemanly manner] Will you allow me to remind you, Mrs Tarleton, that this man has uttered a most serious and disgraceful falsehood concerning Miss Tarleton and myself?

MRS TARLETON. I dont believe a word of it. If the poor lad was there in the Turkish bath, who has a better right to say what was going on here than he has? You ought to be ashamed of yourself, Patsy; and so ought you too, Mr Percival, for encouraging her. [Hypatia retreats to the pavilion, and exchanges grimaces with Johnny, shamelessly enjoying Percival's sudden reverse. They know their mother].

PERCIVAL. [gasping] Mrs Tarleton: I give you my word of honor—

MRS TARLETON. Oh, go along with you and your word of honor. Do you think I'm a fool? I wonder you can look the lad in the face after bullying him and making him sign those wicked lies; and all the time you carrying on with my daughter before youd been half an hour in my house. Fie, for shame!

PERCIVAL. Lord Summerhays: I appeal to you. Have I done the correct thing or not?

LORD SUMMERHAYS. Youve done your best, Mr Percival. But the correct thing depends for its success on everybody playing the game very strictly. As a single-handed game, it's impossible.

BENTLEY. [suddenly breaking out lamentably] Joey: have you taken Hypatia away from me?

LORD SUMMERHAYS. [severely] Bentley! Bentley! Control yourself, sir.

TARLETON. Come, Mr Percival! the shutters are up on the gentlemanly business. Try the truth.

PERCIVAL. I am in a wretched position. If I tell the truth nobody will believe me.

TARLETON. Oh yes they will. The truth makes everybody believe it.

PERCIVAL. It also makes everybody pretend not to believe it. Mrs Tarleton: youre not playing the game.

MRS TARLETON. I dont think youve behaved at all nicely, Mr Percival.

BENTLEY. I wouldnt have played you such a dirty trick, Joey. [Struggling with a sob] You beast.

LORD SUMMERHAYS. Bentley: you must control yourself. Let me say at the same time, Mr Percival, that my son seems to have been mistaken in regarding you either as his friend or as a gentleman.

PERCIVAL. Miss Tarleton: I'm suffering this for your sake. I ask you just to say that I am not to blame. Just that and nothing more.

HYPATIA. [gloating mischievously over his distress] You chased me through the heather and kissed me. You shouldnt have done that if you were not in earnest.

PERCIVAL. Oh, this is really the limit. [Turning desperately to Gunner] Sir: I appeal to you. As a gentleman! as a man of honor! as a man bound to stand by another man! You were in that Turkish bath. You saw how it began. Could any man have behaved more correctly than I did? Is there a shadow of foundation for the accusations brought against me?

GUNNER. [sorely perplexed] Well, what do you want me to say?

JOHNNY. He has said what he had to say already, hasnt he? Read that paper.

GUNNER. When I tell the truth, you make me go back on it. And now you want me to go back on myself! What is a man to do?

PERCIVAL. [patiently] Please try to get your mind clear, Mr Brown. I pointed out to you that you could not, as a gentleman, disparage a lady's character. You agree with me, I hope.

GUNNER. Yes: that sounds all right.

PERCIVAL. But youre also bound to tell the truth. Surely youll not deny that.

GUNNER. Who's denying it? I say nothing against it.

PERCIVAL. Of course not. Well, I ask you to tell the truth simply and unaffectedly. Did you witness any improper conduct on my part when you were in the bath?

GUNNER. No, sir.

JOHNNY. | Then what do you mean by saying that— |

HYPATIA. | Do you mean to say that I— |

BENTLEY. | Oh, you are a rotter. Youre afraid—

TARLETON. [rising] Stop. [Silence]. Leave it at that. Enough said. You keep quiet, Johnny. Mr Percival: youre whitewashed. So are you, Patsy. Honors are easy. Lets drop the subject. The next thing to do is to open a subscription to start this young man on a ranch in some far country thats accustomed to be in a disturbed state. He—

MRS TARLETON. Now stop joking the poor lad, John: I wont have it. Has been worried to death between you all. [To Gunner] Have you had your tea?

GUNNER. Tea? No: it's too early. I'm all right; only I had no dinner: I didnt think I'd want it. I didnt think I'd be alive.

MRS TARLETON. Oh, what a thing to say! You mustnt talk like that.

JOHNNY. Hes out of his mind. He thinks it's past dinner-time.

MRS TARLETON. Oh, youve no sense, Johnny. He calls his lunch his dinner, and has his tea at half-past six. Havnt you, dear?

GUNNER. [timidly] Hasnt everybody?

JOHNNY. [laughing] Well, by George, thats not bad.

MRS TARLETON. Now dont be rude, Johnny: you know I dont like it. [To Gunner] A cup of tea will pick you up.

GUNNER. I'd rather not. I'm all right.

TARLETON. [going to the sideboard] Here! try a mouthful of sloe gin.

GUNNER. No, thanks. I'm a teetotaler. I cant touch alcohol in any form.

TARLETON. Nonsense! This isnt alcohol. Sloe gin. Vegetarian, you know.

GUNNER. [hesitating] Is it a fruit beverage?

TARLETON. Of course it is. Fruit beverage. Here you are. [He gives him a glass of sloe gin].

GUNNER. [going to the sideboard] Thanks. [he begins to drink it confidently; but the first mouthful startles and almost chokes him]. It's rather hot.

TARLETON. Do you good. Dont be afraid of it.

MRS TARLETON. [going to him] Sip it, dear. Dont be in a hurry. Gunner sips slowly, each sip making his eyes water.

JOHNNY. [coming forward into the place left vacant by Gunner's visit to the sideboard] Well, now that the gentleman has been attended to, I should like to know where we are. It may be a vulgar business habit; but I confess I like to know where I am.

TARLETON.I dont. Wherever you are, youre there anyhow. I tell you again, leave it at that.

BENTLEY. I want to know too. Hypatia's engaged to me.

HYPATIA. Bentley: if you insult me again—if you say another word, I'll leave the house and not enter it until you leave it.

JOHNNY. Put that in your pipe and smoke it, my boy.

BENTLEY. [inarticulate with fury and suppressed tears] Oh! Beasts! Brutes!

MRS TARLETON. Now dont hurt his feelings, poor little lamb!

LORD SUMMERHAYS. [very sternly] Bentley: you are not behaving well. You had better leave us until you have recovered yourself. Bentley goes out in disgrace, but gets no further than half way to the pavilion door, when, with a wild sob, he throws himself on the floor and begins to yell.

MRS TARLETON. | [running to him] Oh, poor child, | poor child! Dont cry, duckie: | he didnt mean it: dont cry. |

LORD SUMMERHAYS| Stop that infernal noise, sir: do you | hear? Stop it instantly. |

JOHNNY. | Thats the game he tried on me. | There you are! Now, mother! | Now, Patsy! You see for yourselves. |

HYPATIA. | [covering her ears] Oh you little | wretch! Stop him, Mr Percival. Kick him. |

TARLETON.| Steady on, steady on. Easy, Bunny, easy.

LINA. Leave him to me, Mrs Tarleton. Stand clear, please. She kneels opposite Bentley; quickly lifts the upper half of him from the ground; dives under him; rises with his body hanging across her shoulders; and runs out with him.

BENTLEY. [in scared, sobered, humble tones as he is borne off] What are you doing? Let me down. Please, Miss Szczepanowska— [they pass out of hearing]. An awestruck silence falls on the company as they speculate on Bentley's fate.

JOHNNY. I wonder what shes going to do with him.

HYPATIA. Spank him, I hope. Spank him hard.

LORD SUMMERHAYS. I hope so. I hope so. Tarleton: I'm beyond measure humiliated and annoyed by my son's behavior in your house. I had better take him home.

TARLETON. Not at all: not at all. Now, Chickabiddy: as Miss Lina has taken away Ben, suppose you take away Mr Brown for a while.

GUNNER. [with unexpected aggressiveness] My name isnt Brown. [They stare at him: he meets their stare defiantly, pugnacious with sloe gin; drains the last drop from his glass; throws it on the sideboard; and advances to the writing table]. My name's Baker: Julius Baker. Mister Baker. If any man doubts it, I'm ready for him.

MRS TARLETON. John: you shouldnt have given him that sloe gin. It's gone to his head.

GUNNER. Dont you think it. Fruit beverages dont go to the head; and what matter if they did? I say nothing to you, maam: I regard you with respect and affection. [Lachrymosely] You were very good to my mother: my poor mother! [Relapsing into his daring mood] But I say my name's Baker; and I'm not to be treated as a child or made a slave of by any man. Baker is my name. Did you think I was going to give you my real name? Not likely. Not me.

TARLETON. So you thought of John Brown. That was clever of you.

GUNNER. Clever! Yes: we're not all such fools as you think: we clerks. It was the bookkeeper put me up to that. It's the only name that nobody gives as a false name, he said. Clever, eh? I should think so.

MRS TARLETON. Come now, Julius—

GUNNER. [reassuring her gravely] Dont you be alarmed, maam. I know what is due to you as a lady and to myself as a gentleman. I regard you with respect and affection. If you had been my mother, as you ought to have been, I should have had more chance. But you shall have no cause to be ashamed of me. The strength of a chain is no greater than its weakest link; but the greatness of a poet is the greatness of his greatest moment. Shakespear used to get drunk. Frederick the Great ran away from a battle. But it was what they could rise to, not what they could sink to, that made them great. They werent good always; but they were good on their day. Well, on my day—on my day, mind you—I'm good for something too. I know that Ive made a silly exhibition of myself here. I know I didnt rise to the occasion. I know that if youd been my mother, youd have been ashamed of me. I lost my presence of mind: I was a contemptible coward. But [slapping himself on the chest] I'm not the man I was then. This is my day. Ive seen the tenth possessor of a foolish face carried out kicking and screaming by a woman. [To Percival] You crowed pretty big over me. You hypnotized me. But when you were put through the fire yourself, you were found wanting. I tell you straight I dont give a damn for you.

MRS TARLETON. No: thats naughty. You shouldnt say that before me.

GUNNER. I would cut my tongue out sooner than say anything vulgar in your presence; for I regard you with respect and affection. I was not swearing. I was affirming my manhood.

MRS TARLETON. What an idea! What puts all these things into your head?

GUNNER. Oh, dont you think, because I'm a clerk, that I'm not one of the intellectuals. I'm a reading man, a thinking man. I read in a book—a high class six shilling book—this precept: Affirm your manhood. It appealed to me. Ive always remembered it. I believe in it. I feel I must do it to recover your respect after my cowardly behavior. Therefore I affirm it in your presence. I tell that man who insulted me that I dont give a damn for him. And neither I do.

TARLETON.I say, Summerhays: did you have chaps of this sort in Jinghiskahn?

LORD SUMMERHAYS. Oh yes: they exist everywhere: they are a most serious modern problem.

GUNNER. Yes. Youre right. [Conceitedly] I'm a problem. And I tell you that when we clerks realize that we're problems! well, look out: thats all.

LORD SUMMERHAYS. [suavely, to Gunner] You read a great deal, you say?

GUNNER. Ive read more than any man in this room, if the truth were known, I expect. Thats whats going to smash up your Capitalism. The problems are beginning to read. Ha! We're free to do that here in England. What would you do with me in Jinghiskahn if you had me there?

LORD SUMMERHAYS. Well, since you ask me so directly, I'll tell you. I should take advantage of the fact that you have neither sense enough nor strength enough to know how to behave yourself in a difficulty of any sort. I should warn an intelligent and ambitious policeman that you are a troublesome person. The intelligent and ambitious policeman would take an early opportunity of upsetting your temper by ordering you to move on, and treading on your heels until you were provoked into obstructing an officer in the discharge of his duty. Any trifle of that sort would be sufficient to make a man like you lose your self-possession and put yourself in the wrong. You would then be charged and imprisoned until things quieted down.

GUNNER. And you call that justice!

LORD SUMMERHAYS. No. Justice was not my business. I had to govern a province; and I took the necessary steps to maintain order in it. Men are not governed by justice, but by law or persuasion. When they refuse to be governed by law or persuasion, they have to be governed by force or fraud, or both. I used both when law and persuasion failed me. Every ruler of men since the world began has done so, even when he has hated both fraud and force as heartily as I do. It is as well that you should know this, my young friend; so that you may recognize in time that anarchism is a game at which the police can beat you. What have you to say to that?

GUNNER. What have I to say to it! Well, I call it scandalous: thats what I have to say to it.

LORD SUMMERHAYS. Precisely: thats all anybody has to say to it, except the British public, which pretends not to believe it. And now let me ask you a sympathetic personal question. Havnt you a headache?

GUNNER. Well, since you ask me, I have. Ive overexcited myself.

MRS TARLETON. Poor lad! No wonder, after all youve gone through! You want to eat a little and to lie down. You come with me. I want you to tell me about your poor dear mother and about yourself. Come along with me. [She leads the way to the inner door].

GUNNER. [following her obediently] Thank you kindly, madam. [She goes out. Before passing out after her, he partly closes the door and stops an the landing for a moment to say] Mind: I'm not knuckling down to any man here. I knuckle down to Mrs Tarleton because shes a woman in a thousand. I affirm my manhood all the same. Understand: I dont give a damn for the lot of you. [He hurries out, rather afraid of the consequences of this defiance, which has provoked Johnny to an impatient movement towards him].

HYPATIA. Thank goodness hes gone! Oh, what a bore! WHAT a bore!!! Talk, talk, talk!

TARLETON. Patsy: it's no good. We're going to talk. And we're going to talk about you.

JOHNNY. It's no use shirking it, Pat. We'd better know where we are.

LORD SUMMERHAYS. Come, Miss Tarleton. Wont you sit down? I'm very tired of standing. [Hypatia comes from the pavilion and takes a chair at the worktable. Lord Summerhays takes the opposite chair, on her right. Percival takes the chair Johnny placed for Lina on her arrival. Tarleton sits down at the end of the writing table. Johnny remains standing. Lord Summerhays continues, with a sigh of relief at being seated.] We shall now get the change of subject we are all pining for.

JOHNNY. [puzzled] Whats that?

LORD SUMMERHAYS. The great question. The question that men and women will spend hours over without complaining. The question that occupies all the novel readers and all the playgoers. The question they never get tired of.

JOHNNY. But what question?

LORD SUMMERHAYS. The question which particular young man some young woman will mate with.

PERCIVAL. As if it mattered!

HYPATIA. [sharply] Whats that you said?

PERCIVAL. I said: As if it mattered.

HYPATIA. I call that ungentlemanly.

PERCIVAL. Do you care about that? you who are so magnificently unladylike!

JOHNNY. Look here, Mr Percival: youre not supposed to insult my sister.

HYPATIA. Oh, shut up, Johnny. I can take care of myself. Dont you interfere.

JOHNNY. Oh, very well. If you choose to give yourself away like that—to allow a man to call you unladylike and then to be unladylike, Ive nothing more to say.

HYPATIA. I think Mr Percival is most ungentlemanly; but I wont be protected. I'll not have my affairs interfered with by men on pretence of protecting me. I'm not your baby. If I interfered between you and a woman, you would soon tell me to mind my own business.

TARLETON. Children: dont squabble. Read Dr Watts. Behave yourselves.

JOHNNY. Ive nothing more to say; and as I dont seem to be wanted here, I shall take myself off. [He goes out with affected calm through the pavilion].

TARLETON. Summerhays: a family is an awful thing, an impossible thing. Cat and dog. Patsy: I'm ashamed of you.

HYPATIA. I'll make it up with Johnny afterwards; but I really cant have him here sticking his clumsy hoof into my affairs.

LORD SUMMERHAYS. The question is, Mr Percival, are you really a gentleman, or are you not?

PERCIVAL. Was Napoleon really a gentleman or was he not? He made the lady get out of the way of the porter and said, "Respect the burden, madam." That was behaving like a very fine gentleman; but he kicked Volney for saying that what France wanted was the Bourbons back again. That was behaving rather like a navvy. Now I, like Napoleon, am not all one piece. On occasion, as you have all seen, I can behave like a gentleman. On occasion, I can behave with a brutal simplicity which Miss Tarleton herself could hardly surpass.

TARLETON. Gentleman or no gentleman, Patsy: what are your intentions?

HYPATIA. My intentions! Surely it's the gentleman who should be asked his intentions.

TARLETON. Come now, Patsy! none of that nonsense. Has Mr Percival said anything to you that I ought to know or that Bentley ought to know? Have you said anything to Mr Percival?

HYPATIA. Mr Percival chased me through the heather and kissed me.

LORD SUMMERHAYS. As a gentleman, Mr Percival, what do you say to that?

PERCIVAL. As a gentleman, I do not kiss and tell. As a mere man: a mere cad, if you like, I say that I did so at Miss Tarleton's own suggestion.

HYPATIA. Beast!

PERCIVAL. I dont deny that I enjoyed it. But I did not initiate it. And I began by running away.

TARLETON. So Patsy can run faster than you, can she?

PERCIVAL. Yes, when she is in pursuit of me. She runs faster and faster. I run slower and slower. And these woods of yours are full of magic. There was a confounded fern owl. Did you ever hear the churr of a fern owl? Did you ever hear it create a sudden silence by ceasing? Did you ever hear it call its mate by striking its wings together twice and whistling that single note that no nightingale can imitate? That is what happened in the woods when I was running away. So I turned; and the pursuer became the pursued.

HYPATIA. I had to fight like a wild cat.

LORD SUMMERHAYS. Please dont tell us this. It's not fit for old people to hear.

TARLETON. Come: how did it end?

HYPATIA. It's not ended yet.

TARLETON. How is it going to end?

HYPATIA. Ask him.

TARLETON. How is it going to end, Mr Percival?

PERCIVAL. I cant afford to marry, Mr Tarleton. Ive only a thousand a year until my father dies. Two people cant possibly live on that.

TARLETON. Oh, cant they? When I married, I should have been jolly glad to have felt sure of the quarter of it.

PERCIVAL. No doubt; but I am not a cheap person, Mr Tarleton. I was brought up in a household which cost at least seven or eight times that; and I am in constant money difficulties because I simply dont know how to live on the thousand a year scale. As to ask a woman to share my degrading poverty, it's out of the question. Besides, I'm rather young to marry. I'm only 28.

HYPATIA. Papa: buy the brute for me.

LORD SUMMERHAYS. [shrinking] My dear Miss Tarleton: dont be so naughty. I know how delightful it is to shock an old man; but there is a point at which it becomes barbarous. Dont. Please dont.

HYPATIA. Shall I tell Papa about you?

LORD SUMMERHAYS. Tarleton: I had better tell you that I once asked your daughter to become my widow.

TARLETON.[to Hypatia] Why didnt you accept him, you young idiot?

LORD SUMMERHAYS. I was too old.

TARLETON. All this has been going on under my nose, I suppose. You run after young men; and old men run after you. And I'm the last person in the world to hear of it.

HYPATIA. How could I tell you?

LORD SUMMERHAYS. Parents and children, Tarleton.

TARLETON. Oh, the gulf that lies between them! the impassable, eternal gulf! And so I'm to buy the brute for you, eh?

HYPATIA. If you please, papa.

TARLETON. Whats the price, Mr Percival?

PERCIVAL. We might do with another fifteen hundred if my father would contribute. But I should like more.

TARLETON. It's purely a question of money with you, is it?

PERCIVAL. [after a moment's consideration] Practically yes: it turns on that.

TARLETON. I thought you might have some sort of preference for Patsy, you know.

PERCIVAL. Well, but does that matter, do you think? Patsy fascinates me, no doubt. I apparently fascinate Patsy. But, believe me, all that is not worth considering. One of my three fathers (the priest) has married hundreds of couples: couples selected by one another, couples selected by the parents, couples forced to marry one another by circumstances of one kind or another; and he assures me that if marriages were made by putting all the men's names into one sack and the women's names into another, and having them taken out by a blindfolded child like lottery numbers, there would be just as high a percentage of happy marriages as we have here in England. He said Cupid was nothing but the blindfolded child: pretty idea that, I think! I shall have as good a chance with Patsy as with anyone else. Mind: I'm not bigoted about it. I'm not a doctrinaire: not the slave of a theory. You and Lord Summerhays are experienced married men. If you can tell me of any trustworthy method of selecting a wife, I shall be happy to make use of it. I await your suggestions. [He looks with polite attention to Lord Summerhays, who, having nothing to say, avoids his eye. He looks to Tarleton, who purses his lips glumly and rattles his money in his pockets without a word]. Apparently neither of you has anything to suggest. Then Patsy will do as well as another, provided the money is forthcoming.

HYPATIA. Oh, you beauty, you beauty!

TARLETON. When I married Patsy's mother, I was in love with her.

PERCIVAL. For the first time?

TARLETON. Yes: for the first time.

PERCIVAL. For the last time?

LORD SUMMERHAYS. [revolted] Sir: you are in the presence of his daughter.

HYPATIA. Oh, dont mind me. I dont care. I'm accustomed to Papa's adventures.

TARLETON.[blushing painfully] Patsy, my child: that was not—not delicate.

HYPATIA. Well, papa, youve never shewn any delicacy in talking to me about my conduct; and I really dont see why I shouldnt talk to you about yours. It's such nonsense! Do you think young people dont know?

LORD SUMMERHAYS. I'm sure they dont feel. Tarleton: this is too horrible, too brutal. If neither of these young people have any—any—any—

PERCIVAL. Shall we say paternal sentimentality? I'm extremely sorry to shock you; but you must remember that Ive been educated to discuss human affairs with three fathers simultaneously. I'm an adult person. Patsy is an adult person. You do not inspire me with veneration. Apparently you do not inspire Patsy with veneration. That may surprise you. It may pain you. I'm sorry. It cant be helped. What about the money?

TARLETON. You dont inspire me with generosity, young man.

HYPATIA. [laughing with genuine amusement] He had you there, Joey.

TARLETON.I havnt been a bad father to you, Patsy.

HYPATIA. I dont say you have, dear. If only I could persuade you Ive grown up, we should get along perfectly.

TARLETON. Do you remember Bill Burt?

HYPATIA. Why?

TARLETON.[to the others] Bill Burt was a laborer here. I was going to sack him for kicking his father. He said his father had kicked him until he was big enough to kick back. Patsy begged him off. I asked that man what it felt like the first time he kicked his father, and found that it was just like kicking any other man. He laughed and said that it was the old man that knew what it felt like. Think of that, Summerhays! think of that!

HYPATIA. I havnt kicked you, papa.

TARLETON. Youve kicked me harder than Bill Burt ever kicked.

LORD SUMMERHAYS. It's no use, Tarleton. Spare yourself. Do you seriously expect these young people, at their age, to sympathize with what this gentleman calls your paternal sentimentality?

TARLETON.[wistfully] Is it nothing to you but paternal sentimentality, Patsy?

HYPATIA. Well, I greatly prefer your superabundant vitality, papa.

TARLETON.[violently] Hold your tongue, you young devil. The young are all alike: hard, coarse, shallow, cruel, selfish, dirty-minded. You can clear out of my house as soon as you can coax him to take you; and the sooner the better. [To Percival] I think you said your price was fifteen hundred a year. Take it. And I wish you joy of your bargain.

PERCIVAL. If you wish to know who I am—

TARLETON.I dont care a tinker's curse who you are or what you are. Youre willing to take that girl off my hands for fifteen hundred a year: thats all that concerns me. Tell her who you are if you like: it's her affair, not mine.

HYPATIA. Dont answer him, Joey: it wont last. Lord Summerhays, I'm sorry about Bentley; but Joey's the only man for me.

LORD SUMMERHAYS. It may—

HYPATIA. Please dont say it may break your poor boy's heart. It's much more likely to break yours.

LORD SUMMERHAYS. Oh!

TARLETON.[springing to his feet] Leave the room. Do you hear: leave the room.

PERCIVAL. Arnt we getting a little cross? Dont be angry, Mr Tarleton. Read Marcus Aurelius.

TARLETON. Dont you dare make fun of me. Take your aeroplane out of my vinery and yourself out of my house.

PERCIVAL. [rising, to Hypatia] I'm afraid I shall have to dine at the Beacon, Patsy.

HYPATIA. [rising] Do. I dine with you.

TARLETON. Did you hear me tell you to leave the room?

HYPATIA. I did. [To Percival] You see what living with one's parents means, Joey. It means living in a house where you can be ordered to leave the room. Ive got to obey: it's his house, not mine.

TARLETON. Who pays for it? Go and support yourself as I did if you want to be independent.

HYPATIA. I wanted to and you wouldnt let me. How can I support myself when I'm a prisoner?

TARLETON. Hold your tongue.

HYPATIA. Keep your temper.

PERCIVAL. [coming between them] Lord Summerhays: youll join me, I'm sure, in pointing out to both father and daughter that they have now reached that very common stage in family life at which anything but a blow would be an anti-climax. Do you seriously want to beat Patsy, Mr Tarleton?

TARLETON. Yes. I want to thrash the life out of her. If she doesnt get out of my reach, I'll do it. [He sits down and grasps the writing table to restrain himself].

HYPATIA. [coolly going to him and leaning with her breast on his writhing shoulders] Oh, if you want to beat me just to relieve your feelings—just really and truly for the fun of it and the satisfaction of it, beat away. I dont grudge you that.

TARLETON.[almost in hysterics] I used to think that this sort of thing went on in other families but that it never could happen in ours. And now— [He is broken with emotion, and continues lamentably] I cant say the right thing. I cant do the right thing. I dont know what is the right thing. I'm beaten; and she knows it. Summerhays: tell me what to do.

LORD SUMMERHAYS. When my council in Jinghiskahn reached the point of coming to blows, I used to adjourn the sitting. Let us postpone the discussion. Wait until Monday: we shall have Sunday to quiet down in. Believe me, I'm not making fun of you; but I think theres something in this young gentleman's advice. Read something.

TARLETON.I'll read King Lear.

HYPATIA. Dont. I'm very sorry, dear.

TARLETON. Youre not. Youre laughing at me. Serve me right! Parents and children! No man should know his own child. No child should know its own father. Let the family be rooted out of civilization! Let the human race be brought up in institutions!

HYPATIA. Oh yes. How jolly! You and I might be friends then; and Joey could stay to dinner.

TARLETON. Let him stay to dinner. Let him stay to breakfast. Let him spend his life here. Dont you say I drove him out. Dont you say I drove you out.

PERCIVAL. I really have no right to inflict myself on you. Dropping in as I did—

TARLETON. Out of the sky. Ha! Dropping in. The new sport of aviation. You just see a nice house; drop in; scoop up the man's daughter; and off with you again. Bentley comes back, with his shoulders hanging as if he too had been exercised to the last pitch of fatigue. He is very sad. They stare at him as he gropes to Percival's chair.

BENTLEY. I'm sorry for making a fool of myself. I beg your pardon. Hypatia: I'm awfully sorry; but Ive made up my mind that I'll never marry. [He sits down in deep depression].

HYPATIA. [running to him] How nice of you, Bentley! Of course you guessed I wanted to marry Joey. What did the Polish lady do to you?

BENTLEY. [turning his head away] I'd rather not speak of her, if you dont mind.

HYPATIA. Youve fallen in love with her. [She laughs].

BENTLEY. It's beastly of you to laugh.

LORD SUMMERHAYS. Youre not the first to fall today under the lash of that young lady's terrible derision, Bentley. Lina, her cap on, and her goggles in her hand, comes impetuously through the inner door.

LINA. [on the steps] Mr Percival: can we get that aeroplane started again? [She comes down and runs to the pavilion door]. I must get out of this into the air: right up into the blue.

PERCIVAL. Impossible. The frame's twisted. The petrol has given out: thats what brought us down. And how can we get a clear run to start with among these woods?

LINA. [swooping back through the middle of the pavilion] We can straighten the frame. We can buy petrol at the Beacon. With a few laborers we can get her out on to the Portsmouth Road and start her along that.

TARLETON.[rising] But why do you want to leave us, Miss Szcz?

LINA. Old pal: this is a stuffy house. You seem to think of nothing but making love. All the conversation here is about love-making. All the pictures are about love-making. The eyes of all of you are sheep's eyes. You are steeped in it, soaked in it: the very texts on the walls of your bedrooms are the ones about love. It is disgusting. It is not healthy. Your women are kept idle and dressed up for no other purpose than to be made love to. I have not been here an hour; and already everybody makes love to me as if because I am a woman it were my profession to be made love to. First you, old pal. I forgave you because you were nice about your wife.

HYPATIA. Oh! oh! oh! Oh, papa!

LINA. Then you, Lord Summerhays, come to me; and all you have to say is to ask me not to mention that you made love to me in Vienna two years ago. I forgave you because I thought you were an ambassador; and all ambassadors make love and are very nice and useful to people who travel. Then this young gentleman. He is engaged to this young lady; but no matter for that: he makes love to me because I carry him off in my arms when he cries. All these I bore in silence. But now comes your Johnny and tells me I'm a ripping fine woman, and asks me to marry him. I, Lina Szczepanowska, MARRY him!!!!! I do not mind this boy: he is a child: he loves me: I should have to give him money and take care of him: that would be foolish, but honorable. I do not mind you, old pal: you are what you call an old—ouf! but you do not offer to buy me: you say until we are tired—until you are so happy that you dare not ask for more. That is foolish too, at your age; but it is an adventure: it is not dishonorable. I do not mind Lord Summerhays: it was in Vienna: they had been toasting him at a great banquet: he was not sober. That is bad for the health; but it is not dishonorable. But your Johnny! Oh, your Johnny! with his marriage. He will do the straight thing by me. He will give me a home, a position. He tells me I must know that my present position is not one for a nice woman. This to me, Lina Szczepanowska! I am an honest woman: I earn my living. I am a free woman: I live in my own house. I am a woman of the world: I have thousands of friends: every night crowds of people applaud me, delight in me, buy my picture, pay hard-earned money to see me. I am strong: I am skilful: I am brave: I am independent: I am unbought: I am all that a woman ought to be; and in my family there has not been a single drunkard for four generations. And this Englishman! this linendraper! he dares to ask me to come and live with him in this rrrrrrrabbit hutch, and take my bread from his hand, and ask him for pocket money, and wear soft clothes, and be his woman! his wife! Sooner than that, I would stoop to the lowest depths of my profession. I would stuff lions with food and pretend to tame them. I would deceive honest people's eyes with conjuring tricks instead of real feats of strength and skill. I would be a clown and set bad examples of conduct to little children. I would sink yet lower and be an actress or an opera singer, imperilling my soul by the wicked lie of pretending to be somebody else. All this I would do sooner than take my bread from the hand of a man and make him the master of my body and soul. And so you may tell your Johnny to buy an Englishwoman: he shall not buy Lina Szczepanowska; and I will not stay in the house where such dishonor is offered me. Adieu. [She turns precipitately to go, but is faced in the pavilion doorway by Johnny, who comes in slowly, his hands in his pockets, meditating deeply].

JOHNNY. [confidentially to Lina] You wont mention our little conversation, Miss Shepanoska. It'll do no good; and I'd rather you didnt.

TARLETON. Weve just heard about it, Johnny.

JOHNNY. [shortly, but without ill-temper] Oh: is that so?

HYPATIA. The cat's out of the bag, Johnny, about everybody. They were all beforehand with you: papa, Lord Summerhays, Bentley and all. Dont you let them laugh at you.

JOHNNY. [a grin slowly overspreading his countenance] Well, theres no use my pretending to be surprised at you, Governor, is there? I hope you got it as hot as I did. Mind, Miss Shepanoska: it wasnt lost on me. I'm a thinking man. I kept my temper. Youll admit that.

LINA. [frankly] Oh yes. I do not quarrel. You are what is called a chump; but you are not a bad sort of chump.

JOHNNY. Thank you. Well, if a chump may have an opinion, I should put it at this. You make, I suppose, ten pounds a night off your own bat, Miss Lina?

LINA. [scornfully] Ten pounds a night! I have made ten pounds a minute.

JOHNNY. [with increased respect] Have you indeed? I didnt know: youll excuse my mistake, I hope. But the principle is the same. Now I trust you wont be offended at what I'm going to say; but Ive thought about this and watched it in daily experience; and you may take it from me that the moment a woman becomes pecuniarily independent, she gets hold of the wrong end of the stick in moral questions.

LINA. Indeed! And what do you conclude from that, Mister Johnny?

JOHNNY. Well, obviously, that independence for women is wrong and shouldnt be allowed. For their own good, you know. And for the good of morality in general. You agree with me, Lord Summerhays, dont you?

LORD SUMMERHAYS. It's a very moral moral, if I may so express myself. Mrs Tarleton comes in softly through the inner door.

MRS TARLETON. Dont make too much noise. The lad's asleep.

TARLETON. Chickabiddy: we have some news for you.

JOHNNY. [apprehensively] Now theres no need, you know, Governor, to worry mother with everything that passes.

MRS TARLETON. [coming to Tarleton] Whats been going on? Dont you hold anything back from me, John. What have you been doing?

TARLETON. Bentley isnt going to marry Patsy.

MRS TARLETON. Of course not. Is that your great news? I never believed she'd marry him.

TARLETON. Theres something else. Mr Percival here—

MRS TARLETON. [to Percival] Are you going to marry Patsy? PERCIVAL [diplomatically] Patsy is going to marry me, with your permission.

MRS TARLETON. Oh, she has my permission: she ought to have been married long ago.

HYPATIA. Mother!

TARLETON. Miss Lina here, though she has been so short a time with us, has inspired a good deal of attachment in—I may say in almost all of us. Therefore I hope she'll stay to dinner, and not insist on flying away in that aeroplane.

PERCIVAL. You must stay, Miss Szczepanowska. I cant go up again this evening.

LINA. Ive seen you work it. Do you think I require any help? And Bentley shall come with me as a passenger.

BENTLEY. [terrified] Go up in an aeroplane! I darent.

LINA. You must learn to dare.

BENTLEY. [pale but heroic] All right. I'll come.

LORD SUMMERHAYS| No, no, Bentley, impossible. I | shall not allow it. |

MRS TARLETON. | Do you want to kill the child? He shant go.

BENTLEY. I will. I'll lie down and yell until you let me go. I'm not a coward. I wont be a coward.

LORD SUMMERHAYS. Miss Szczepanowska: my son is very dear to me. I implore you to wait until tomorrow morning.

LINA. There may be a storm tomorrow. And I'll go: storm or no storm. I must risk my life tomorrow.

BENTLEY. I hope there will be a storm.

LINA. [grasping his arm] You are trembling.

BENTLEY. Yes: it's terror, sheer terror. I can hardly see. I can hardly stand. But I'll go with you.

LINA. [slapping him on the back and knocking a ghastly white smile into his face] You shall. I like you, my boy. We go tomorrow, together.

BENTLEY. Yes: together: tomorrow.

TARLETON. Well, sufficient unto the day is the evil thereof. Read the old book.

MRS TARLETON. Is there anything else?

TARLETON. Well, I—er [he addresses Lina, and stops]. I—er [he addresses Lord Summerhays, and stops]. I—er [he gives it up]. Well, I suppose—er—I suppose theres nothing more to be said.

HYPATIA. [fervently] Thank goodness!

9 789389 155556

Printed by Libri Plureos GmbH in Hamburg,
Germany